F. JACO

HE C

The Confessions
of Josef Baisz

The Confessions of Josef Baisz

A NOVEL BY
DAN JACOBSON

SECKER & WARBURG : LONDON

First published in England 1977 by
Martin Secker & Warburg Limited
14 Carlisle Street, London W1V 6NN

Copyright © Dan Jacobson 1977

SBN: 436 22045 8

Printed and bound in Great Britain by
Morrison & Gibb Ltd, London and Edinburgh

Translator's Preface

THE READER OF this extraordinary autobiography will want to know how it came into my possession. I can tell him exactly.

It was brought to me without preliminary notice, one rainy Saturday afternoon, by a complete stranger. He simply rang on my door-bell, asked for me by name, and said that he had come to me at the suggestion of "a mutual friend" in Bailaburg. He had a letter for me from that friend. I invited him in and he took off his sodden raincoat. Only then did I notice the parcel he had been carrying under his arm.

The letter from my friend, whom I had not seen since I had left the Republic of Sarmeda and returned to London a couple of years before, was brief and very guarded. Indeed it was unsigned. It said merely that "Mr 'S Koudenhoof" would be bringing me "a small present" which I might be able "to make some use of". That was all. I opened the parcel and saw the typescript inside. When I questioned my visitor about this unsolicited gift, he answered evasively, even mockingly, standing in the middle of my living-room and mopping his brow and moustache with a hand-kerchief that soon became as damp as the rest of him. What was it? The autobiography of a scoundrel, recently deceased. What was I to do with it? Translate it into English. My friend had said that I could do the job. And then? Find a publisher. And his interest in it? Oh, he had no interest in it, certainly no financial interest. He just thought it would be "amusing" to have it published. It would "serve them right". Whom did he mean? Read it and see. And if I didn't want to undertake the task? He would find somebody else who did.

Drenched, slight, solitary, youthful in his gestures and bearing, middle-aged (at least) around the eyes and mouth, my visitor was remarkably self-possessed. Now that I have read these *Confessions* I wish that I could question him about his own part in them, and about how he managed to get hold of the copy he left with me. (As well as about the fate of the other copies which the author mentions.) But I have not seen him since. He has not called back, as he said he would, to find out whether or not I was interested in doing the translation. He stayed with me for about twenty minutes only. During that time he said that he would probably be in London for another week or two. Then he would be travelling again. No, not back to the Republic. He was finished there. If they ever laid their hands on him –! Perhaps he would be better off in Latin America. Perhaps not. He would get in touch with me, anyway.

That was the end of our conversation. Declining my offer of a cup of tea, he donned his raincoat, turned up its collar, and plunged down the watery path. The rain was still falling steadily. I watched him until he was out of sight.

Naturally, when I sat down to read the typescript the first question I asked myself was whether or not the story it told was true. I suppose the conclusion I came to is obvious from the fact that I am now offering this translation to English-speaking readers. But I admit that I have no irrefutable evidence, either at first hand or from other sources, of the veracity of the tale. During my three years in the Republic, as Lecktor in English at the Bailaburg Institute of Comparative Linguistics, I met none of the people whom Josef Baisz mentions in his *Confessions*. The fact that I lived through some of the political upheavals he writes about, and can recognise the accuracy of his descriptions of certain streets, buildings, and landscapes, is not really significant one way or the other. My visitor, as I have said, has not made himself available for further questioning. Nor have my researches into newspaper files been of much assistance in verifying the story. For example, I have confirmed that the ruler of the Republic did indeed visit Volmaran Island about nine months ago, as Josef Baisz describes in the latter section of the memoir. I have also found an account in the *Boschoff Courant* of the trial to which he alludes towards the end. But the existence of these reports does not – and cannot, in itself – corroborate what Josef Baisz tells us about his relationship to the events they describe.

Moreover, an enquiry I addressed to the Sarmedan Embassy in London elicited the following reply, which I transcribe verbatim:

> Your letter of ———— is not the first indication we have had that a vicious forgery, purporting to be an "autobiography" or "confession" of a certain "Josef Baisz", is being circulated both within the Republic and in countries with which it maintains friendly relations. We are sure that this malign invention will be seen by all truth-loving people for what it is. The contradictions and implausibilities in the document are manifest. However, in order to avoid any ambiguity or misunderstanding, the Government of the Republic wishes to declare explicitly that is has no record of the birth of any such citizen as Josef Baisz – let alone of his having achieved high office in the service of the state. The bankrupt and degenerate elements responsible for this impudent slander of our country are well known to us, and the Government of the Republic will do all it can to see that they are brought to justice. In the meantime it regards with the utmost gravity the readiness of some foreign governments to permit these vile plotters and besmirchers, and their local hirelings, to continue their nefarious activities.

So where does that leave the reader? Compelled, quite simply, to judge the text for himself. He must form his own impression of Josef Baisz. He must ask whether he can recognise any of his own motives – in a grossly distorted form, no doubt – in Baisz's account of the impulses which drove him through his career as bodyguard, police-spy, kidnapper, murderer, and favoured son of the regime. My own view of the matter, strengthened by my knowledge of conditions inside the Republic, is clear. The torments Josef Baisz inflicts upon himself and others; the spasmodic pleasures he enjoys; the urgency of his compulsion to confess his misdeeds and thus in some measure to make amends for them; his climb to, and rapid fall from, a position of some eminence in the ramshackle dictatorship which governs his country; his revelation of the opportunities which such a regime offers to its people, and of the corruptions which they bring in their train – all these, I am convinced, have the unmistakable stamp of truth upon them. I need hardly add that in coming to this conclusion I am far from being animated by any feelings of hostility to the Republic. Whatever my opinion of its rulers may be, I have nothing but affection for the people and country evoked so vividly in the following pages.

A few terms in the text have been left untranslated from the original; none of them will present any difficulty to the English or American reader. It remains for me to thank the Foundation for the Defence of Free Speech for a small grant that enabled me to complete this translation; the staff of the British Museum (Newspaper Section) in Colindale for their unfailing helpfulness; my colleagues at the North End Polytechnic, particularly those in the Geography Department, for the patience they have shown with my queries; and my publishers for the support I have had from them throughout. My greatest debt is to my wife, without whose linguistic skills this translation would be less satisfactory than it is. I am, of course, wholly responsible for any errors which it may contain.

M. D. de B.

4

The Confessions
of Josef Baisz

I

I WAS BORN in the town of Vliss, up in the north. It is a place of no importance. No one goes there, apart from the usual commercial travellers and a few asthmatics. The atmosphere on the plateau is supposed to be good for people with chest complaints.

Next to a wide, muddy river; within a clump of trees; surrounded by lucerne and maize fields; under an enlarged sky . . . there's Vliss. Most of the village is grouped round an unpaved square; the rest of it straggles along the main road, or lies at the end of obscure double-tracks. Vegetable patches and iron sheds abound. Beyond, to the north, the earth is flat; it shows of itself only what the onlooker sees immediately around him. The southern horizon is broken by the blue and mauve ridges of the Middelbergen; occasionally the even more distant white peaks and slopes of the Hoogbergen become just visible, like a tent-city improbably moored in mid-air. Directly overhead there is space enough for all the world's clouds to come and go as they please.

There were advantages in growing up in a place like Vliss. I know the names of birds, trees, and wild flowers. I learned at an early age how to shoot and how to ride a horse. I get on well with dogs. What I plant, grows.

But the greatest advantage of having spent my childhood there was that it made me so eager to get away! It filled me with longings for scenes different from those I already knew: the wide, melancholy sunsets of a flat country, silent but for the piping of a hidden bird; passenger trains moving across dark fields at midnight, like so many visionary streets; roads and fences always about to start the trek to remote horizons; the stare of strangers, wondering at the improbable conjunction of their lives with mine; telegraph poles vibrating as they passed on their messages, while the wind moaned to be let into the secret. Had such sights and sounds not made a daydreamer of me I would never have been impelled into action. Had I not felt so acutely my own insignificance, I would never have tried so hard to do anything about it.

Enough coarse paradoxes, for the moment. Now for some simple facts. Beginning with the family, where we all begin.

My father: an official in the Maize Industry Production Board. Therefore, a civil servant. A weigher. A checker. A man with a pencil behind his ear and the keys to the Board's storehouse in his pocket. The farmers of the district were compelled by law to bring their maize crop to the storehouse; according to instructions he received from the provincial capital these stocks were then either railed away or milled locally. The mill, also a state concern, was managed by our cousin Felix. He was a busybody, a rural district councillor, and a zealous member of the Phalanx of Democratic Control.

My mother: a shopkeeper in the village square. She sold sweets, cigarettes, shoelaces, small toys, and similar articles. The shop was tiny; so was its turnover. In its window was an embossed card on which were affixed dummy packets of cigarettes, the lettering on them so faded you could hardly make out their brand-names. (Some of the very first words I learned to read: *Sweet Secrets*, *Tricolor*, *Sport*, *Gazelle*.) You had to step down to get into the shop, and keep your head lowered, once you were inside it. We lived behind and above the shop. Our landlord was a local magnate, who owned a bar and a garage in the village, as well as a farm several kilometres out of town. After my father was arrested he helped the family by lowering the rent. I think he had his eye on my older sister.

My father was taken away to be tried in Boschoff, together with

Cousin Felix. This was during the period of P.P.E. (Production, Planning, Expansion); and a particularly grave view was taken by the authorities of crimes against state enterprises. Felix and my father were accused of falsifying documents and embezzling money. My father had invoiced Felix for maize which the latter never received and never milled, but for which the state paid nevertheless. They were supposed to have shared the profits of this simple peculation.

We stayed with some relations in Boschoff while the trial was on. It was the first big town I had ever visited, and it seemed a very imposing place to me. Of all I saw there, the size of the shop-windows impressed me most; I had never imagined that in one place there could be so many large, unbroken expanses of glass, reflecting and revealing so much. But I was also excited by street-lamps, tall buildings, long streets, and the passing to and fro of people whom I would never meet again. In the cobbled central square, the Plaas, where we sat on benches and ate rolls out of paper bags, tram-cars gathered side by side and head to head, like animals in a paddock; I listened as if to music to the amazing variety of sounds they produced. All round were public buildings: the City Hall, the Provincial Prefect's palace, the main post office, the Magistratuur. Stationary bronze lions and ever-mobile flocks of pigeons guarded the flights of steps that led up to them; great stone hoods protected their windows; greenish roofs of copper, streaked with black, sat on top of them like skull-caps.

Within the Magistratuur (white walls and bland shadows) officials whispered and handed each other papers, a man in the witness-box talked of invoice numbers and weighbridge tickets, a woman moved her lips and fingers over a machine with an incomprehensibly small number of keys, while a narrow never-ending roll of paper emerged jerkily from it and fell into a special receptacle at her side. The judge spoke of the trust that had been betrayed, of the grave times through which the country was passing, of the need for all citizens to be alert to corruption, of duty and deterrence. My mother sighed; Cousin Felix sat with his head between his hands; my father swallowed convulsively

9

and kept his eyes on the judge. The pock-marks on his face looked almost purplish in hue. When he was asked if he had anything to say before being sentenced, he accused Felix of having suggested the scheme to him, and of having kept the proceeds of it for himself; Felix said the same about him. They were both found guilty and were sentenced to five years' hard labour apiece. Felix was given an extra year in prison for bringing grave dishonour on the Phalanx. Then they disappeared down a staircase immediately behind the dock.

Later that same day we rode in a tram-car for a long time, until we reached a prison, or series of prisons, on the outskirts of town. We presented passes at a gate and walked up a gravelled drive, accompanied by a man in uniform. We were not taken into the immense stone building ahead of us, but to an iron-roofed bungalow standing on its own; one of several scattered about the grounds. It reminded me vaguely of the little schoolhouse in Vliss. After a long wait my father was brought in. He no longer looked as he had in the courtroom, when he had been stiffly, even fanatically attentive and apprehensive throughout. He had passed beyond his own terror since then. He told us why, his eyes glistening with a manic self-assurance, a fatal hilarity. "I won't be locked up for five years," he said. "I won't be locked up for one. I'll be dead before then." He spoke of his death as of a treat he was promising himself. "You'll see." He kissed us in turn and went out between the two men who had brought him in, supported by neither. I had never felt prouder of him. He was so brave. Having been taken out of the forsaken, humdrum sphere in which he had always lived, and translated into one graver, more dignified, more metropolitan, more consequential in every way, he was showing himself fully worthy of it.

He was as good as his word. He hanged himself in his cell just two or three months after he had been sent to a work-prison in the Petrus district.

On our return from Boschoff I spent many hours looking for the money which, in childish fashion, I felt sure my father must have hidden somewhere about the house. I looked under loose floorboards in the attic, behind pieces of furniture that hadn't been moved for years; I examined the drains in the little yard behind the shop. But I had no luck. Though I no longer had easy access to the Maize Board's storehouse, I managed to get inside it one Sunday and spent almost the whole afternoon looking for some possible place of concealment among the stacked bags. Heavy, stiff, slippery, they were too much for me; I was just a boy of twelve. But I did my best; I persisted until horizontal rays from the setting sun came in through the storehouse eaves, lighting up myriads of motes that struggled to escape from the glare, and died the moment they succeeded.

I found nests of mice in the shed; a woman's dress and hairnet hidden inexplicably under some empty bags; even a two-kirat coin in a pile of dust. But of real money, of the money I was looking for, not a trace. It was then, in the grain-scented silence of my father's place of work, conscious both of his presence and absence, that I cried for the last time in my life. It was then, also, that I vowed not to be taken by surprise again, if I could possibly help it. To do better than my father. To know more about others than they knew about me. In short, to make something of my life.

I have already mentioned some of the advantages of growing up in a place like Vliss. Another, quite the opposite of what most people would assume, was that we suffered less from my father's disgrace and suicide than we might have done in a big city. Because everybody knew what had happened, there was nothing for us to hide. Therefore, no lies; no skeletons in the cupboard; no possibility of being overtaken by the past and disgraced anew. Anyway, there wasn't a family in Vliss that hadn't suffered an equally public disgrace at some time or another: a murder, an illegitimacy, a madness, a drunkenness, a theft, an idiot discovered bound in a shed, an act of wartime collaboration or treachery . . . So while people enjoyed our disgrace to the utmost, of course, they were careful not to make too much of it in our presence, by a display either of sympathy or malice. The one exception to this was Felix's son, Anton, who was a couple of years older than myself, and was determined to let everyone see just how much of a righteous grievance he had against me and my family. Accordingly, when we were swimming in the river he stuck my head under the water and held it there until the muddy swirl I had seen going under turned into a thunderous, explosive blackness, streaked with lightning and blood, from which it still surprises me I ever managed to emerge. He and some of the boys in his class pulled my trousers down and displayed my weedy growth in front of the girls. He peed on my schoolbooks and trod them in the dust. Though we all knew he was a little cracked – it could be seen in his remote, pale eyes; heard in the vacant caw of his laughter – there was nothing original about his mind, or the torments it managed to devise. Then he joined the Boys' Brigade and left the village. I was to meet him again, years later, in very different circumstances.

At home, things were rather difficult. My mother had always been indolent and melancholy: a fatal combination of qualities, each having so much to offer in support of the other. She had also been prone to histrionic rollings of her eyes, wistful catchings of her breath, and brief outbursts of gaiety. All this, together with her thin, almost breastless figure, her somewhat squinting gaze, and her fondness for frilly underwear, had choked me and made me hot to please, filled me with forebodings and longings, throughout my boyhood. After my father's death she became worse in every respect, and I fell out of love with her; I found her merely tiresome and predictable. When my sisters didn't cook, we ate cold; when they didn't sweep, dust and disorder accumulated. The younger of the two girls, Beata, did all the work in the shop; the older one, the pretty one, went to work in the Monopol Hotel. She didn't stay there for many months. She left with one of the commercial travellers who frequented the place – an elongated pedlar of hardware, of whose brown suit with reddish stripes I have a clear memory. When we heard from my sister it was from Boschoff, then from Slaipklipp, in the south, on the other side of the mountains; then from the distant capital, Bailaburg; then not at all.

Skinny, sharp-faced Beata remained behind. Poor Beata! She

was always the last to sit down to a meal and the first to get up from it. My mother fell into ever more protracted silences, punctuated with spells of mirth and grief; she also developed a horror of the wide spaces of the square just outside the shop. Time went by. Now it was summer, now winter. On summer evenings people sat out in the square on kitchen chairs; in winter, stoves ticked and roared, the colour of their enamel tops changed as if with emotion, steam trickled down the insides of windows. People attended services in the little white-walled Bethanian chapel, as the authorities wished them to, then watched the weekly cinema show in the village hall. What else can I wax lyrical and reminiscent over, so many years later? That every autumn we watched the mounted Kuni tribesmen, in their multi-coloured blankets and wide straw hats, driving their cattle on the long trek down from the Middelbergen towards the winter grazing-grounds which our enlightened government carefully preserved for them? That on Settlement Day all the children were given sponge-cake and lemonade at school, and the grown-ups got drunk in the evenings? That we were taken into Vanir by coach, during the agricultural show, to see a team of French dare-devils turning their cars over and over, and hurling their bikes over pits of flame?

There is an iron law that applies to people who live in places like Vliss. The wider their horizons, the narrower their minds.

Two anecdotes, then, to conclude this section of my memoirs. They will at least illustrate how little capable I was of rising above my Vliss background.

First anecdote. Featuring a stripy kitten. It sails through the air and strikes its side against the wall of one of the upstairs rooms. The other members of my family are perhaps at church or visiting the next-door neighbours; I don't know where. No matter. The stripy kitten is alone with me. It is hanging against the wall as if skewered there or suspended from above. Its back is arched, its legs and tail hang downwards. Then it slithers down, still against the wall, like rain or paint. It lands on four paws, next to the wainscoting. It begins to walk in the direction it is facing, without knowing where it is going, or why. There is something tottery about its walk, like that of a new-born calf or lamb. I reach out a hand to pick it up, to show it that I had never intended to harm it. My hand is just a child's, but the kitten fits easily into it. It seems to open its whole face to mew at me, revealing a tongue and teeth too small to be dangerous; they are like jewels, or like the internal organs of a flower. A moment later, foolishly, in rag-like fashion, with one leg stretched out in the sack of its own skin, it is sailing through the air, towards the wall. A remarkable sight. Someone is panting; it can hardly be me, because I have exerted myself so little; it cannot be the cat, because it is too small to make so loud a noise. After a while the kitten learns to try to avoid me, but it is too small and too dazed to be able to do so. It has to flow down the wall several times before it manages to disappear through the open door. I lie down on the bed and feel my heart beating right through my body, through the bed, the floor, the house, the whole square.

The second story is perhaps in even worse taste than the last, though that may seem hardly possible. This time I am accompanied by a schoolmate of mine, Luis. Luis's mother has "Kuni blood", and therefore neither she, nor her husband, nor Luis himself, are what you would call highly regarded in the community. Luis and I are at the bottom of the smallholding farmed by Luis's father; there is a smell of pig in the air and a field of cabbages immediately behind us; in front of us is a small stream. We are stretched out full-length on the damp ground, hidden by a growth of cow-parsley and alder. Luis's penis is in my left hand; mine is in his right hand. We are both fully clothed; our bodies hardly touch; only our flies are open. What makes Luis's cock so exciting to hold is not its warmth and smoothness, wonderful though they are, or the simplicity and cunning of its form, ditto; but, mysteriously enough, the fact that it feels thinner in my hand than my own does in his. Perhaps the same mystery works in reverse for him. We do not discuss the matter. I have my hand over my eyes; when I take it away, I see branches and leaves quite without substance in the sudden flare of colourless light revealed to me; some time has to pass before the leaves become green and the sky blue and gold. Then I cover my eyes once more. I don't know how long we lie like that. Forever.

The experience with the kitten was never repeated. That with Luis many times. I was kind to the kitten before and after it. Luis I was always unkind to, away from the bank of the stream. Nobody knew we were friends. In fact, we weren't friends. I called him "Kuni-creeper" like all the other boys at school, and gave him a rougher time in the schoolyard and elsewhere than most. In my kindness to the cat there remained the sweet, poison drop of what I had once done to it. In my bullying of Luis there was always the dizziness of complicity, of knowing that in a day or a week we would meet in secrecy once again, to put each other through the same silken, remorseless pleasure as before.

II

FROM SCHOOL I went straight into the office of Frans Kitzinger. All his titles – commission agent, appraiser, negociant, prockureur, etc. – were painted in thick gold letters with black shading across the window of his office on the village square. In the window there was also a large china vase, containing the inevitable pair of dead flies.

I stayed with Mr Kitzinger for three years. I learned to type; I picked up some business jargon; I acquired the rudiments of book-keeping and office routines. Some of these skills proved to be of use to me subsequently. Of even greater profit were the hours I spent in the office when I had no duties of any kind to perform. On one of the shelves above the safe stood a twenty-volume set of the Universal Library of Famous Literature, in imitation leather and gilt bindings, in which I browsed extensively while Mr Kitzinger drove about the district looking for business. The books contained passages (in translation) of everyone from Addison to Zeno. Sometimes, when even Mr Kitzinger couldn't keep up the pretence of being constantly in demand by his clients, he would entertain me by reading his favourite extracts aloud, with gestures.

On my nineteenth birthday I received notification that I had been balloted for call-up into the Republican Guard. I was alone in the office when the postman brought me the letter, and I didn't tell Mr Kitzinger about it. In the evening, after closing the doors of the office, I walked out of the village, along the main road to Vanir. The sun was setting, and a thin, spectrally white crescent of a moon had already appeared. A couple of kilometres down the road there were some cattle-pens where auctions were held every quarter-day. I sat on the top rail of one of the pens and looked back the way I had come. The colour of the moon changed from white to silver; from silver to gold. One by one the lights of the village appeared. They were so thinly scattered over so wide an area, it was impossible not to pity them. Never again would they mark the bounds of my life.

Suddenly I could no longer bear either their loneliness or my own. I got down from the fence and ran back to the village. The moon bounded along with me, like a good-humoured puppy. I went into Pieck's bar and ordered a brandy, and told everyone where I was going to be in a week's time. At home I didn't break the news to Beata and my mother until I'd gone into the bedroom and written a kind of poem in one of my old school exercise books. It went like this.

> *The future has blue eyes.*
> *Its face is unlined, but its hair*
> *is already grey.*
> *It looks straight at me,*
> *as if it knows me well.*

Then I felt much better; no longer so frightened. I promised Beata I would write to her regularly.

To the accompaniment of harsh discords – yells and farts, snores and stamping feet – my memory throws out next a succession of disconnected pictures in bewildering close-up. The wall of a wooden hut. A face distorted by the shout it is producing. A hand (mine) trembling as it lifts a mug of tea. Shadows of legs crossways on the bare earth. A blanket. Sky. More sky. A red-dyed granolithic step with cracks like rivers on a map running

17

across its surface. Naked men with black, wet heads in a steaming shower-room.

For a moment, or for a few hours, the confusion settles. We are in the oval hall of the Old Drostdy in Boschoff, taking an oath of loyalty to the Republic of Sarmeda and its beloved Heerser. Our voices rise in chorus, just as when we had rehearsed the ceremony in camp; but here they produce a furry, indeterminate echo which is trapped under the moulded white ceiling and in the arched recesses of the windows. The floor beneath us, amazingly enough, is of sand. Outside are black cupolas and white colonnades; gilded lettering in incomprehensible Latin running along every frieze; gravelled courtyards and black, wrought-iron gates. After the ceremony we are allowed to wander through the building, gaping in this direction and that. Someone says that the floor of the great hall is sanded because that's where they used to carry out executions in the olden days. With an axe. With the king and queen looking on. Someone else says that the Colonel-Commandant of the Guard is "the hell-in" with our O.C. training for some reason I can no longer recall. Soon we are put back into buses. Boschoff is left behind. Our voices rise in melancholy chorus once more.

> *Your thighs are wet,*
> *Your thighs are flat,*
> *Your thighs are easy to get at,*
> *Thighs, thighs, thighs . . .*
> *How do your thighs feel now?*

The camp again. Confusion again. Random noise and images. Time bereft of meaning, apart from its division into periods for drill, P.T., meals, showers, route marches, lectures, sleep, rising to drill again. Every day exactly like the others, even Sunday. Every view from the perimeter of the camp showing the same bald countryside, over which the sun mechanically rises and sets, as if it is only out of a sense of duty that it visits this dejected, unpeopled part of the country.

Within it all, at the very centre of dislocation and discomfort,

18

I become aware of a pair of shining brown eyes fixed with a curious blank intensity upon me. They belong to my company commander, Captain Serle. Of him more shortly. Much more.

Out of it all, there emerges a happiness I had hoped for and am yet surprised by. A sense of peace. A desire to remain where I am. Thinking of Vliss, I no longer feel the pain of homesickness. I have another home, among these men and huts, inside this barbed-wire fence. I even have a special friend, whose company I seek out in my spare time. His name is Fenter: a reserved, athletic fellow, the son of a schoolmaster in a village not far from Vliss. He excels in our games of football and bock-bock. He has a large head with a wide, calm brow like a statue's, concealing the moodiness and ambition within. We drink together in the camp beer-hall. We go together to films in the camp cinema. I hear about his quarrels with his parents. About his younger brother, who is "brilliant". About his own ambitions. He even tells me that he writes poetry, though he shows me none of it.

Then a break: our first spell of leave.

I went home, of course, like everyone else, and found the place even quieter and emptier than I had remembered it to be.

When the villagers asked me how things were going in the army, I answered proudly, "I'm not in the army, I'm in the Guard."

When they asked me what it was like in the Guard, I answered even more proudly, "Tough!"

Even Mr Kitzinger looked at me with a respectful eye, and laughed uneasily when I reminded him of our literary afternoons in his office. Beata fingered the buttons on my tunic, and marvelled at the weight and shininess of my boots. Only my mother wasn't impressed by my new uniform and new status. She insisted on speaking of me as a policeman, though I patiently explained to her that service in the Republican Guard had nothing to do with petty crime. Everyone knew that. We represented the central power of the state. We were the army of the interior, so to speak. Our business was with strikes, riots, army mutinies, prison breakouts, guerrilla activities, uprisings among the Kuni or Sedi . . .

She interrupted this summary of the many lectures we'd been given on the nature of our duties. "You're a policeman, it's no good saying you aren't."

"And you're a fool!" I shouted at her. "It's no good pretending you aren't."

Whereupon her jeers turned instantly into tears. Of the two, I preferred her tears, just at that moment. But they also made me feel how much better off I was in camp than at home.

Before going on leave I had arranged to meet Fenter at the railway station in Vanir, and to travel back with him to camp. Now I persuaded Beata to come with me as far as Vanir; I wanted to show off one of my new companions to her. The three of us walked up and down the station platform together. It was a warm evening. Insects fell from the lights suspended in the black hollow of the roof. Fenter's boots and mine crunched gratifyingly on the concrete. The door of the station buffet groaned and clattered melodramatically, like an actor rehearsing a death, every time anybody entered or left. Beata and Fenter were shy with one another at first, as I had expected them to be; but they soon warmed up. In an affected, highflown manner which was new to me, Beata talked about "the sufferings we have gone through as a family", and asked Fenter if he did not long for a "better order of things". He replied that he did. To prove it, presumably, he began making fun of the Guard, the Phalanx, and the Heerser. I had never heard him talk in that fashion before. Then the train to carry Beata back to Vliss pulled in. The shaded lights of its carriages made an intimacy of every seat and luggage-rack. "Take care of yourselves," she said from the train window. She looked like an old woman, sharp nose foremost, head-scarf knotted under her chin. Fenter was touched to be included in her injunction. "I'll look after him," he assured her. She waved until the carriage was out of sight. His voice a little higher than usual, Fenter told me that I was lucky to have such a nice sister.

Later, while our train travelled northwards through the darkness, Fenter asked me what Beata had meant when she'd spoken of the sufferings my family had gone through. I told him about my father's imprisonment and suicide. Though I couldn't be sure of it because of the dim light in the compartment, I thought his eyes were glistening by the time I came to the end of my tale.

"Didn't it make you feel bitter?" he asked.

"Against what?"

"Everything. The whole world."

I looked through the window. All I could see out there was my reflection and Fenter's, with a gleaming light above them: two suspended, imperfect creatures, through whom dark space streamed endlessly.

"No, not really," I answered.

"Why not?"

"My father knew what he was taking on. He must have known. That's how he made a man of himself, in the end. You know what I think? Everything's double. And double again. Even God needs the devil to make something of himself."

The wheels of the train hammered fiercely, the carriage swayed freely, I stretched myself out on the bunk and fell asleep to their contrasting rhythms. When I opened my eyes in the morning, I knew at once what I must do to act on what I had said to Fenter.

It wasn't difficult. Once we were back in camp I signed a docket asking for permission to see Captain Serle privately. This was a right all of us had, in terms of the regulations. An appointment was given to me for the following morning.

Stamp. Salute. I met his stare. Not a trim figure, our company commander, behind his desk. A deep chest. A big head. A rumpled uniform. Pale reddish hair, cut short. Freckled skin. A small, hoarse voice. Blank, bright, expressionless eyes.

"Yes –" consulting the paper in front of him, "yes – Baisz – what is it?"

I hesitated, I stammered, I told him that someone in Company D, a friend of mine, had been talking disloyally about the Guard, the Phalanx, and even about the Heerser. I didn't want to get my friend into trouble and hoped to be told that such talk didn't matter. But I felt it my duty to report the conversation, nevertheless.

He let me wait before he spoke. Then: "Your friend's name is – ?"

"Must I tell you, sir?"

"Yes."

"Fenter, sir."

"All right, Baisz. Thank you. You can go."

"And in the future, sir?"

"Just use your discretion."

"Thank you, sir."

Salute. Stamp. About turn.

Afterwards I felt – purified. There's no other word for it. As though I had confessed my own misdeeds, not Fenter's. Strong, too. Full of charity. When I saw Fenter I loved him for his ignorance of what I had done to him.

Everyone had got Judas wrong! That was my great discovery. When he pressed his lips to the master's, he did it passionately, with a breaking heart and an expectant eye, full of excitement and curiosity, trembling with pity at the thought of the suffering his victim would soon have to undergo. He hadn't done it for the sake of the silver. Never. He was one of those who loved only what he betrayed; who could love only through betrayal.

I was another.

It now seems extraordinary to me that I should have been able to think of myself in such terms without despair, without terror. What a fate! What a role! Didn't I remember what Judas was driven to subsequently? Couldn't I understand it to have been the last spasm of a process begun long before?

Well, I know it now. At the time, however, my discovery merely left me feeling rather complacent and self-admiring, like a young man who had just learned that he had a real talent for mathematics, say, or one of the arts.

Serle summoned me back to his office about a week after I had first called on him. He told me he was appointing me recreations organiser – lectures, raffles, cinema shows, etc – for the company.

That was to be my reward. Also, my cover. I was to return to him with any further tales I might pick up about people in the company.

In the weeks that followed I discovered that he wasn't greatly interested in hearing about anti-government talk of the kind Fenter had indulged in. What my company commander – that remote, terrifying figure, vested in my eyes with all the authority of the state – what he really wanted from me was gossip. Nothing less. Nothing more. How the men talked about him among themselves. How they talked about the other officers. Whether any of the other officers spoke approvingly or slightingly of him, Serle.

He listened to my stories with an absorbed, smooth expression on his face, like that of a child sucking its thumb. His bright eyes were lowered. More. More. I did my best. When I hadn't enough titbits of information to give to him, I used to make them up. Major Hansen had accused his wife of being a whore. Sergeant Kramp had said he was going to kill Eybers. And so on. Serle took no notes. He never thanked me for my information. The intensity of our sessions together was matched only by their pointlessness. The afternoon's warmth was trapped in the office. From outside I could hear the noise of vehicles and distant cries from the parade ground. Five minutes. Ten minutes. Occasionally fifteen. That was all. No more. I would go out, exhausted. In the front office the clerks eyed me suspiciously.

The weeks passed. Our training went forward. Soon we would be sent to stations all over the country. One night in the camp beer-hall – at our feet a litter of the empty wax-paper cartons in which the special army brew was sold; between us a slopped-upon trestle-table – I heard from Fenter that some of the men in the company were accusing me of being Serle's moff. His trass. His hasie . . . The usual variety of epithets, all meaning the same thing.

"They're pretty worked up about it," Fenter told me. "They say they're going to do you over."

"Who?"

"Gouws. Helfrich. Smart."

He looked about the bleak, hangar-like building, uneasy at having given me these names. After a silence he went on: "I've told them to leave you alone. I've said that you're all right."

"Thank you."

Fenter smiled, but his blue eyes remained troubled. He was worried for me. He was also worried, I could see, for himself. Who would want to be the best friend of Serle's moff?

"You're scared they'll do you in too?" I challenged him.

He coloured and his eyes shone more brightly. But he didn't deny it. "I told them to leave you alone," he said again.

"I'll get them. Bastards. You wait and see."

It was an empty threat. But the chance to get at one of them, at least, came soon; and in unexpected fashion. Gouws was the one involved: a lumbering, flat-headed booby, given to spells of uncontrollable excitement that practically anything could set off. Gouws the louse, we used to call him; then he would run mad.

My chance came about like this. We were at the seventy-five metre range one morning, taking turns at firing ten rounds rapid and ten rounds deliberate at stationary targets. It was a familiar exercise, which I always enjoyed. I liked its contrasts. You peered through a black hutch into an oblong of light where the target stood in foreshortened view. You concentrated intensely during your periods of firing, and then stood or lay about in complete idleness during the longer spells of waiting. The noise of the shots was deafening; so was the silence of the countryside, which re-asserted itself during every protracted pause. Even the inter-mittent thuds from a mortar range somewhere beyond the horizon – as of giant, invisible doors slamming in the sky – merely made more poignant the blue stillness overhead.

About half-way through we were joined by Captain Serle, who arrived in an open command-car that had come bouncing along the double-track from the camp. He looked no more trim in the field, our company commander, than he did behind his desk. His belly was more in evidence. His thighs rubbed together with every stride he took. Above – a single stare. Behind – a red, cropped neck, bulging out over the stiff collar of his tunic. Beneath the activity of an officer doing his duty – boredom, disdain, ambition.

The subalterns told him that everything was in order; the sergeants said the same; those of the men whom he asked about their performance smiled bashfully, some because their scores were high, some because they were low. Gouws, who had been lying on the ground a little distance from the rest of us, got to his feet when Serle approached. He was holding his rifle by its sling. Serle did not ask him his score. As he turned to go back to the command-car, Gouws jumped in front of him, grinning from ear to ear, like an excited dog.

"Ninety-three, one-two-seven, ninety-eight," he yelped out. "Sir."

Serle smiled faintly; not unkindly, one might have thought. He brought up his swagger-stick and touched Gouws's neck with it, just below the Adam's apple. The lithe little cane bent under the pressure before it sprang free. It was as if Gouws were simply a piece of trash to be flicked aside. Serle continued on his way to the car. With some effort he swung himself into it. The driver started the engine.

Gouws's intrusion had been impertinent; Serle's dismissal of it contemptuous; the whole incident had been commonplace. Gouws stood with his hand to his neck, where the cane had touched him. He was motionless, staring ahead; he seemed quite stupefied by what had happened. Yet nothing had happened. People were turning away, many of them slumping back on the ground. I was about to do so myself, when I saw Gouws's whole face throb blindly: once, then again, like a pulse. I looked in the direction of the car and was surprised to see how near it still was. It seemed hardly to have moved. The rear tyres went over a bump; the stencilled number-plate, hanging down from the back, shivered separately from the rest of the vehicle. His dog-grin once again splitting his face, Gouws brought up his rifle and aimed it at Serle.

Do I believe, re-telling the story now, that he intended to fire? No, I do not. Did I believe it then? Not really. Nevertheless I made the lunge that changed my life. "Look out!" I yelled at the top of my voice and grabbed at the rifle from the side. It wasn't Gouws with whom I found myself wrestling, but the rifle itself. Its strength was phenomenal. It tore at the sockets of my arms. It got away from me and flew into the air. With an inconsequential, grating, squeaking noise, it banged against my head. The noise was nothing, the darkness it produced all-enveloping. When I recovered consciousness, Gouws was a few metres away, with men hanging on to him by every limb and around the neck. The whole group was writhing incoherently to and fro. People were running from every direction. There was a babble of voices. Serle was there, too. Someone took Gouws's rifle, and pulled back the bolt. There was a cartridge in the breech. It was carried like that, with great solemnity, and presented to Serle for his inspection.

Gouws's pleas, cries, tear-sodden assertions and denials, some of them abject, some stupidly defiant, do not need to be described. He played his part admirably. He was packed off to a military prison after a summary enquiry at which I modestly recounted what I had seen and done. For my trouble I received a handshake and a word of commendation from the O.C. of the camp, as well as a slightly more emotional version of the same from Serle. Thereafter none of the men in the company spoke of doing me over because of my meetings with him.

Our passing-out parade was a big day. Members of our families were invited to attend. Beata came in a red dress and pale stockings she had purchased for the occasion, and walked about with her arm through mine, like a lady. Fenter, with whom my relations had been a little strained since our conversation in the beer-hall, neglected his parents in order to be fatuously attentive to her.

III

MANY MONTHS LATER I was stationed at a place with the euphonious native name of Dong-dong, up in the mountains, when a message came for me to report to the Deputy-Minister of National Guidance in the capital. No explanation was given of the message. I didn't know who the minister was, let alone his deputy.

It was one of those periods – well, one of those periods when names and faces you are in the habit of seeing day after day in the newspapers suddenly disappear from them. When small items announce without comment that all the officers of the ————th or ————th Armoured Brigade have been cashiered and put under arrest. When rumours circulate about shootings in this or that provincial city. When the radio constantly broadcasts warnings against saboteurs and enemies of the state, together with appeals to workers in essential industries to ignore the activities of unnamed diversionists. Of course, you know at such times that in the end the Phalanx will emerge from the turmoil purified, strengthened, purged of unhealthy elements; but until the announcements to that effect are made, it is difficult to tell just who those elements will turn out to have been.

In a godforsaken place like Dong-dong we could do no more than read the newspapers that arrived a day later than usual, sometimes with large, unexplained blank spaces in their pages, and listen diligently to the news on the radio. We were kept on permanent stand-by, of course. Bald-headed, weak-minded Lieutenant Alberts, who was in charge of us, waited anxiously for messages from regional headquarters in Klaaris; it was obvious to us that he didn't know whether to be grateful to be stuck safely in Dong-dong at such a time, or sorry to be missing opportunities for distinguishing himself elsewhere. On balance, I think he was glad to be out of the way.

Everything went on pretty much as usual in the bleak, sprawling settlement which our stone and iron fortress overlooked. The Sedi, in my experience, are an inscrutable lot. Their golden skins reflect the light; their eyelids fit with a curious neatness over round black eyes; their narrow mouths run into lugubrious wrinkles. The men sat in front of their stone huts and the women tilled their wretched fields. Our flag hung down immovably in the cold autumn air, as if the frost had already got into it and turned it into a substance stiffer than cloth. The Sedi watched us with rather the same mixture of dependence and scorn as that with which we watched Lieutenant Alberts. "Just let them start anything," we said, fingering our weapons and half-hoping that they might. It would at least have kept us occupied. "Just let them try." But they didn't oblige. The two long, dusty shopping streets of the settlement were as crowded as ever with mule-carts and rattletrap lorries by day, and as deserted by night. On Saturdays the mountain folk for miles round came to attend the Sabbath services in their granite-walled, iron-roofed Bethulian cathedral, and we listened from outside to the unfamiliar chanting and bell-ringing that accompanied their rite. When we went out in the evenings we could hear through closed doors that the Sedi, too, had become very keen on following the news on their radios.

In the middle of all this Lieutenant Alberts called me into his office and showed me the message that had just been passed on to him by telegraph from Klaaris. It was specific and unambiguous. Baisz J., 612907-V was to proceed at once to Klaaris, where a movement warrant awaited him for travel to Bailaburg. There he was to report to the deputy-minister, in person, at the Ministry of National Guidance.

"What have you been up to, Baisz?" Alberts asked, making no effort to disguise his ravenous yet suddenly respectful curiosity.

"I wish I knew, sir," I answered sincerely. The deputy-minister! Bailaburg! Me! I could only assume that I had done something wrong somewhere, at some time, without knowing what it was, and was now going to be punished for it.

Like many bald men, Alberts had the habit of comforting himself, whenever he was troubled, by rubbing the top of his head with the flat of his hand. He did so now, producing a dry, insect-like sound, while his eyes went back and forth between me and the message on the desk. The nearer he drew to a foregone conclusion, the slower became the movement of his hand. Finally it stopped.

"Well, you better go, then."

I was on my way within an hour. I said goodbye to some of the men who were hanging round. Fenter got permission to give me a ride down to Klaaris on the signal company's motor-bike and side-car. The road wound through a soaring, plunging world of peaks and valleys, with screes of tumbled rock dragged apparently at random across the slopes. Water-courses were furred with growth, like the secret parts of a woman. The widest valleys had been ruled off into ploughed fields and were dotted about with cubical stone houses, as if for a giant's board-game. At every hairpin bend in the road a segment of sky and mountain wheeled above us and then righted itself. Out of my fear that I was being called to account for a terrible misdemeanour I didn't even know I had committed, I shouted to Fenter, above the noise of the wind and the motor, "If something does happen to me, try to help Beata as much as you can."

"Of course."

We had travelled some distance – far enough to negotiate a couple of bends – before he leaned his leather-helmeted head towards me and yelled, "You know me and Beata – we've started writing to each other."

"No," I lied, at the top of my voice, "I didn't know." Actually, Beata had told me.

Anyhow, my testament was made. From then on I was mute and passive until at last I stood in the deputy-minister's office, in Bailaburg.

He looked at me across an expanse of green leather and oiled wood.

There was a smile of uneasy pride on his lips. Yet his eyes were as blank as ever.

"Baisz?"

"Yes, sir."

"You remember me?"

"Of course, sir."

"You remember what you did for me?"

I hesitated. "Sir?"

Time for one of his silences. A long one.

"You saved my life from that lunatic Gouws, didn't you?"

"Thank you, sir."

"How would you like to do it again?"

"Sir?"

Another silence. He moved his chair away from the desk, exposing more of himself to view. He was wearing a uniform without insignia or badges of rank. His hands came together just above his belly.

"Have you been following the news?"

"I've been trying to, sir."

"There've been changes, Baisz. Overdue changes. I've helped to make them."

Silence.

"Two companies of the Guard in the right place, at the right time . . . They didn't do everything, but they did something. Enough."

Silence.

"You have a new Colonel-Commandant, you know. I've just helped to appoint him."

At this final boast his lips wrinkled once more into a smile; his eyes did not.

"I want you to be my bodyguard, Baisz. That's why I've sent

for you. I've got to have a man of my own here. Someone I can trust. Who's got no connections with anybody else in Bailaburg. You understand? I don't want to be dependent on others . . . for this. I've studied your record. It's clean. No drink, no gambling, no insubordination. No politics either. You've never been stationed here, which is a great advantage. And you've already shown me that you're – suitable – for the job. In more ways than one."

I listened to these abrupt, amazing sentences; then to the profound silence that followed. The room itself seemed to be attending: its tessellated floor, its tall white walls, its remote ceiling within which writhed and glimmered much green and gilt moulding. The windows behind Serle ran almost the full height of the room, and were surmounted by two coif-like pelmets. He was looking through me, at nothing. I opened my mouth. He began talking again.

Conscientiously. In a tone of what I can only call dutiful fanaticism. It was familiar to me from many places. Even from school. The faces and the voices changed. But not the phrases or the manner in which they were delivered.

Economic crises. Mistakes in certain circles. Management failures. Opposition elements. Regroupings. Uncontrolled personal ambitions. Purification. Renewal. Corruption. Danger from many quarters. Left and right. Vested interests. Treachery. Revenge. Desperation.

Silence.

"That's where you come in, Baisz."

"Yes, sir."

"It's a difficult job. A dangerous one. Highly responsible. Once you take it on, your life's no longer your own. It's mine. Always. You're never off duty." A buzzer on his desk suddenly sounded loudly. With a stiff forefinger that hovered for a moment, then pounced, he struck it dead. "So what's your answer?"

Our eyes met. There was never any doubt in his mind or in mine what my answer would be. Yet we had to go through this additional period of silence: that of a decision being taken.

Whatever followed would then be the result of a choice I had made.

I drew in a breath. "I'll do my best, sir."

He opened a drawer and took out a black automatic pistol clipped into a shoulder holster. The gesture was obviously one he had rehearsed before my arrival. Now the objects lay on the desk between us: leather, webbing, metal. To them, after digging in the drawer again, he added a box of cartridges. He lowered his chin into his neck to indicate that I should pick them up.

"You better get that stuff on. I don't want you showing it off all over the ministry."

There was nowhere for me to put down my cap and tunic except on a little gilded chair in the corner of the room. It seemed a long way to walk, across the echoing black and white tiles. It also seemed to take me an embarrassingly long time to get my tunic off. I slipped the harness over my shoulders and tightened the strap; then I donned my tunic once again. Breathing in, I did not know whether the harness felt like a constriction or support across my chest and shoulders. The holster protruded less than I had thought it would. I put the box of cartridges into the breast-pocket of my tunic and buttoned it up. Serle watched me with much satisfaction.

"Right," he said, when I returned to the desk. He had taken a file out of a drawer, and he began to go through it now, glancing at a different paper each time he made a point. "This is how things stand, Baisz. You've been seconded indefinitely from the Guard. So you must get out of that uniform. Next, you're entered in the ministry's books as my special assistant. Nothing's been put down about your specific duties. That's how I want it. You don't have to say anything about yourself to anyone. Is that clear? Thirdly, you're going to attend a special school at the Burzenack Camp – it's run by the Ministry of Justice, but it's an inter-departmental affair, everybody sends people along. Police, M.P.C., B.S.D., S.C.O.P.P., Compresecor, External Affairs, the lot. You won't be asked questions while you're there and you won't ask them. They'll teach you some clever tricks. I've got a little office booked for you down the corridor: it'll be yours when you come back. That's all. Oh, you'll want some money for your new clothes. And to get to Burzenack. I'll have a voucher made out for you right now. You wait for it, eh? You'll be on the regular pay-roll by the time you come back."

After this long speech he sat breathing effortfully for a while, before pressing one of the buttons on the little array in front of him. The call was answered by an aged, institutional figure in pin-stripe trousers whom I vaguely remembered seeing on my way to Serle's office. It seemed to me that hours had passed since a bemedalled commissionaire had led me along obscure, unswept corridors, cluttered with filing-cabinets and cardboard cartons; into empty chambers glittering with mirrors and raindrop chandeliers; up and down stairways smelling domestically of dinner; past crowds of girls behind rattling typewriters. Now I followed the old man out of the office. His shoulders were bowed, his hands arthritically twisted. When I made as if to close the double doors behind me, he gestured reprovingly. That was his job. He did it with many lobster-like flourishes of his claws. My last glimpse of Serle showed him still to be staring at me. Once the doors were closed, the old man's demeanour changed abruptly. He nudged me with a bony elbow, in friendly fashion, and tilted a rheumy eye at me. Just a fraction further and some of the liquid in it might have overflowed. "This way," he said.

A girl sat at a desk in the antechamber, reading a book. She didn't look up as we went past. The old man led me through an archway, down a long passage, and into a lobby or waiting-room. In a niche in one wall, between two windows, stood a bronze cast of a Greek-style youth, with a leaf over his genitals and a winged helmet on his head. He seemed to be lost in admiration at the smoothness of his left arm. Through an open door I could see part of a landing, and a bloated marble staircase, the colour of cheese. The old man disappeared. I sat down on a polished wooden bench and waited, as he had told me to.

Time passed slowly. Once a secretary tripped down the stairs with much agitation of her bosom. Many minutes later she was followed by two soldiers who were arguing loudly with one another, about what I couldn't make out; both of them had their caps on the back of their heads. I sat there quite numbly. If I felt anything, it was merely relief at having no further demands made of me for the moment.

More footsteps on the marble floor, ringing and knocking: both sounds at once. Across the landing and into the lobby came a man and a woman. Strange though it now seems to say so, what I noticed first about the woman's face was its nakedness. Its cleanness. Its clarity. It was without excess anywhere. Her cropped black hair exposed it. She wore no make-up. There was no down on the olive skin of her cheeks or upper lip. (But that I only found out later.) Her white skirt swayed about her calves as she walked. In a voice and accent which for me had some of the improbable charm of a foreign language – it was so refined, it was so much of the south – she said to her companion, "You'd better wait here, Connie – I'll go and see him." Her large, oval eyes passed over me with no special curiosity. Yet when they swung away it was as if a beam of light had left me. She disappeared through the archway.

The young man sat on one of the chairs opposite me. He stared at me in an embarrassingly direct manner; then tilted his head and stared at the ceiling above us; then scratched at the top of his head with one fingernail, inspected what had become lodged under it, and flicked the offending matter away. I couldn't help admiring him for behaving so casually in such a grand place; also for the slenderness of his feet and hands, and the cut of his double-breasted grey suit.

These southerners! I had never been south of the mountains before, and everyone I had seen since getting off the train had a peculiar metropolitan glamour in my eyes. The south was the part of the country from which our ancestors had set out, centuries before, to conquer the northern, tramontane province; right here in the capital lived the people who produced our laws and books and films. Their imagined existence had always had the power to make our lives, on the wrong side of the mountains, seem almost unreal, wanting in some final quality of seriousness.

So I felt as if the man sitting opposite were virtually a member of a different species. He resembled the woman who had come in with him, but his face didn't have the pure, bland, newly created quality of hers. She had looked as if she had just risen from a cleansing chaos; he was merely pretty. But until I sat on that bench, furtively regarding him, it had simply never occurred to me that a man could be thought of as pretty.

When the rheumy-eyed messenger returned, the young man got to his feet. "I beg your pardon, sir," the messenger apologised, with a placatory wave of his claws; then turned to give me one of his abrupt head-jerks. The other frowned, put out that I had been sent for before him, and I rose with as much of an air of importance as I could assume. To my surprise the messenger led me not to a cashier's office, as I had been expecting him to, but once again to Serle's.

He was standing up, with his back to the tall windows. The woman I had seen outside was sitting in front of his desk. "Come in, come in," he said impatiently, beckoning me forward. "Here he is, Gita. My new bodyguard. Baisz, you'll be seeing a great deal of this lady."

I bowed in her direction. She had turned her head to look at me. The light coming in through the net curtaining was brighter than it had been before, and I could not make out the expression on her face.

"Baisz is a northerner," Serle said. "A country boy. Isn't that right? I got to know him when we were stationed in Kazerne. I picked him out then. He did very well there. Now I'm giving him his chance to prove himself. Baisz" – he addressed me again – "this is Mej. 'S Koudenhoof, my fiancée. We're getting married next week. So you'll have to take good care of her as well."

"You'll have to guard my body, too," she said, in a level, beautiful, indifferent voice.

I was petrified. I didn't know where to look. Serle just snorted. "You could say that."

"I hope he knows his job."

"He's going off to Burzenack to learn it. All right, Baisz, that's all."

I bowed again, feeling the biggest fool in the world. The lady sat with her knees together, her hands in her lap. I backed out of the room. It wasn't until I was following my aged guide down yet another set of corridors that I realised I had not said a single word while I had been in Serle's office. What a dummy I must have appeared!

Later still, sitting in the front seat of a motor-car, holding in my hand the voucher Serle had promised me, I realised that he had also been anxious to make an impression on his fiancée. Indeed, that was why he had sent for me.

The driver of the car was a tough-looking woman of about forty, wearing a dark green uniform. Her name was Eva. She pointed out the sights to me as we drove along. Every avenue presented a different vista, culminating always in a pallid, frowning, corrugated building of state. The Tomb of the Forty-Six. The Court of Cassation. The Chamber of Deputies. The President's Summer Palace, which could be seen through an archway made not of stone but of aspiring, crossing jets from an enormous fountain. The Folckersaal. Everywhere, it seemed, green branches of willow and scaly arms of pine hung over balustraded bridges, which in turn hung over streams of water that ran alongside lawns and rock-gardens, or tumbled foaming down little waterfalls and disappeared underground. Hidden and revealed among the trees on the horizon were the coppery or black domes of the Palace of Justice, the College of Preceptors, the National Museum, the State Opera House, the Hall of the Revolution, the Dome of the War Dead, La Sagesse Cathedral . . .

So many times I had seen pictures of them all; and now here they were, on a scale I could never have imagined; and here I was; and it was in the midst of them I was to live and work. Numb no longer to my good fortune, I was drunk on it. On the visions of grandeur and order around me. On the intimate terms with which I'd been admitted to them.

Eva turned the car through the Raitz Arch, and we left behind all the buildings and gardens of what was called, as I was later to learn, the Kring. The car plunged into the business district of the city. We were instantly surrounded by shops and traffic. Bicycle-bells trilled like birds above all the other noises. I was deposited in front of the State Credit Bank and left there, on my own, to get on with my new life.

IV

TRICHARDT SERLE'S FATHER had been a lawyer in Port Margriet. An ardent member of the Phalanx from his student days, he had commanded a detachment of middle-class youths during the overthrow of the First Republic. Rewarded with a job in the public prosecutor's office, he was in due course promoted to the bench, on which he served to the end of his days. Literally. He was on the point of sentencing a pickpocket to a well-deserved term of imprisonment when he brought his hand to his mouth, opened his eyes wide, and collapsed on to the table in front of him, striking his forehead hard on an elaborate metal inkstand which had been presented to him by the officials of the court just a few months before.

"You see, Baisz," Serle said, pointing out the inkstand to me, in its honoured place in his study, "I come from a family with a tradition of public service. And of loyalty to the Phalanx. These things count. My father died at his post."

"Yes, sir. A very fine end."

By that time Trichardt, the judge's only son, was a cadet at the Military Academy at Belmas. He daydreamed of receiving a colonelcy at an unprecedentedly early age, of having streets named after him before he was thirty, of becoming Heerser at forty, and of retiring to write his memoirs at fifty.

"You understand what I mean, Baisz. I always felt I was

marked out for something different. For doing more. Trying harder. Going higher."

"Quite rightly, sir."

His big opportunity had come just after dawn one morning, on National Route East 3, about forty kilometres from Bailaburg. He was bivouacked on the side of the road with five lorries and a company of about a hundred men, near a place called Ottoskopp, waiting for the further orders which had been promised him by his brigade commander. He knew no more than that "something was up": which was worse than knowing nothing at all. At speed towards him, while he waited, there came a big black car carrying no less a personage than Deputy-Premier Spass, who had also learned that something was up, and was hurrying back to the capital from his farm in the Smidsdriff district to find out more. The car stopped. The deputy-premier beckoned Serle, who recognised him from his photographs, to the car-window. The two men spoke together for a few minutes. Serle turned his trucks round and escorted the deputy-premier back to Bailaburg. From then on he displayed on Spass's behalf all the zeal of a man who has discovered that in the eyes of his senior officers he has done the wrong thing, and who knows what his fate will be should their faction nevertheless triumph. Once the crisis was resolved, several junior and senior ministerial posts were vacant. Serle's loyalty was remembered. Spass's position in the government was stronger than before. The feeling was widespread that as some units of the Guard had been so disgracefully implicated in the upheaval, it would be good for the morale of the corps if one of its officers was given a post in the reformed administration. Soft-spoken, silver-haired Professor Andrie, who had held his portfolio at the Ministry of National Guidance throughout, agreed readily enough.

"I could have arrested Spass, you understand. Imagine that! There was nothing to stop me. I was alone. Everything was silent. Even the fields and trees still looked asleep. But I knew where my duty lay. I chose as my conscience dictated. Rightly – eh? It's easy to say so now. The difference is: I knew it then."

"That's wonderful, sir."

We had such conversations in the car, with Eva silent at the wheel; in his office at the ministry; sometimes on the patio at the back of the house, where he reclined on a swinging, hammock-like couch, with a fringed awning above, while I stood in front of him. I also heard him talking in this vein when he and Mef. Serle entertained people at the house, and I would have to help in the kitchen or with the serving of drinks. That was also part of my duties, it seemed.

In his more despondent moments, however, Serle spoke of his promotion as a sacrifice he had inflicted on himself for the sake of the Republic; of his present position as a martyrdom he endured solely in order to be of service to others.

"Honestly, Baisz, I was never happier than when I was a simple soldier in the Guard. Those were the days! You remember? I had no cares then. But now? I tell you, if I could – if I could bring myself to do it – I'd resign today. This morning."

"You can't do that, sir. You mustn't even think of it. The country needs you."

Whereupon a look of fatuously disinterested consideration would come upon his face, while he earnestly reflected on what I had said. It was an expression that seemed to concentrate itself upon a point just beyond the tip of his straight little nose. Finally, reluctantly, he would agree with me.

"Probably you're right, Baisz," he would sigh. "I suppose I don't have any choice in the matter. Given my character and upbringing."

I wonder, do I make him sound more of a fool than he really was? I hope not. I certainly did not think of him as a fool during my first few months in his service. The idea didn't enter my head. How could it? In that house? In the position he occupied? Surrounded by flunkeys like Hardackker, his first secretary, and "all the other little shits in the front office" (Serle's description)? Driving him to meetings at which the highest in the land would be present? Knowing that I owed everything to him and that without him I would (at best) be flung back into the Guard, losing at a stroke all the excitements and privileges I enjoyed?

Christ!

Let me describe them. The excitements and privileges, I mean. In sequence. In a manner befitting the orderly, punctilious person I tried to become. Beginning, as my new career did, with that school in Burzenack to which Serle had sent me.

The place had come up fully to my incoherent expectations. Any private soldier suddenly catapulted into a position like mine would have been bemused. For a northerner, for someone from Vliss, for a daydreamer, the effect was magical. Nothing, as far as I was concerned, could have improved upon the peeling pilasters and lichenous stonework of the dilapidated country house, once the home of the Burzenack family, in which we lived. The lavish autumnal foliage of the woods all round was a revelation to me; so was the softness of the air and the complexity of the countryside. Having just spent several months in the savage Hoogbergen, I felt it to be almost unfair that such small stretches of territory should present so cultivated a variety of view. Even the lakes and little mountains looked as though they had been deliberately put there with an eye both to use and adornment, like the terraces of fruit-trees and the stone bridges over a multitude of talkative streams.

In this garden of Eden I learned the habits of violence and vigilance which our instructors imparted to us. Shooting at moving and stationary targets from all angles. Entering ambushed rooms. Shadowing suspects through the streets of Burzenack town. Unarmed combat. Emergency drills in cars and on staircases. Recognition of booby traps. Methods of interrogation.

There were about thirty of us going through the course. We slept in bare dormitories upstairs and ate with our instructors in what had once been the hall of the house. On one wall of the dining-room was the usual photograph of the Heerser; on the other an oil-painting of a dejected delegation from beyond the Blauw River signing the Satisfaction of Bailaburg (1653) under the ruddy eye of General Raitz. Sometimes, after dinner, we went out drinking in Burzenack town; other evenings, we carried out exercises.

Happy days. In spite of what Serle had said, most of the trainees were ready enough to tell me the stories of their lives and to talk about the branches of the services they came from or would be going back to, once they had completed the course. There were all sorts among them, of course, but they did have in common certain characteristics which I recognised without difficulty. (And also without dismay.) They were all daydreamers, fantasists, people who sought fulfilment and a sense of their own reality in violence and double-dealing. My *semblables*, my rivals. I listened to them, but kept my own counsel; when they asked me directly what I was doing, I just said that I had been seconded from the Guard. Which was true enough, as far as it went.

On our last night we had a farewell party in the hall. We bombarded each other with bread-rolls, we sang, we played football with somebody's cap, a man called Georges passed out, another man vomited. A night to remember. Then, excitedly, proudly, filled with expectations and apprehensions, determined to make myself indispensable not only to Serle but to the entire administration, I returned to the capital.

Now: a day in the life of a bodyguard. 7 a.m. Rise, go to the back door of the villa and unlock it, so that Manuella and Dirck, the house-servants, can come in from their cottage in the grounds. 8 a.m. Open front door for Eva, who has brought the car. Walk down the drive. Look circumspectly to left and right along the green, empty, dew-bright street, lined with the gardens of villas similar to Serle's. 8.05 a.m. Get into front seat of car; tell Eva which route to follow to the ministry. 8.30 a.m. Climb out of car and scan steps of ministerial palace. Walk with Serle to his office. Take up position in small office down corridor. 8.35 a.m. onwards. Check all arrivals against the list of appointments. Read books and gossip with passers-by. Leave office with Serle at different times, either to go straight home at the end of the day (6.00 p.m. or later) or to attend luncheons and receptions, conferences at other ministries, public meetings and rallies, concerts and plays. Midnight. Check all locks on doors and windows, set burglar alarms, sleep with revolver in cabinet next to my bed.

And the next day:

7 a.m. Rise . . . I slept in a bedroom placed at the main hinge or elbow of the sprawling villa which Serle had received on his appointment to the ministry. On one side of my room were the sleeping quarters and bathrooms; on the other the living-rooms and the large hall. In front of the house was a horseshoe-shaped drive; at the back there were lawns and flower-beds, a sunken swimming-pool, and a border of silver oaks and pines, from which the ring-doves woke me every morning, chanting their dawn devotions. The house was inviolably quiet, surrounded by green-ery; indeed, invaded by greenery. Glass panels had been let into a corner of the roof of the hall, to give light to the tropical plants which grew in pots and urns on the floor of polished brick, as in a conservatory. The grounds were looked after by men from the Ministry of Public Works; Dirck and Manuella did everything else. Their cottage at the end of the garden was a trim, white-washed little place: a childlike dwelling for a childless couple. Manuella took the breakfast trays into the Serles' bedrooms. I seldom saw Mef. Serle before I left in the morning with her husband.

8 a.m. Open front door for Eva . . . Even at that hour she brought with her into the house a black, bitter reek from the cigarettes she incessantly smoked. We were good friends, initially; lovers briefly, despite the difference in age between us; then friends again.

8.05 a.m. Get into car . . . Much depended on the morning mood of Serle, my boss and my charge. Sometimes he was genial and garrulous; at others, snappish. I was always deferential. I felt it was part of my job to be deferential.

8.30 a.m. Arrive at office . . . At first my own presence in and around the ministry and other buildings of state filled me with such incredulity I was convinced I would actually be unrecog-nisable to anyone who had known me previously. How could so great a change in my circumstances not have wrought an equiva-lent change in my appearance? Later, inevitably enough, I began to take the grandeurs around me more for granted. But as long as

43

I remained in Serle's service the feeling that I was playing a part in an elaborate charade never entirely left me.

8.35 a.m. onwards . . . No, I won't list the names of Serle's visitors; there were too many of them. The Ministry of National Guidance was responsible for all the state information services; for the censorship of books, newspapers and films, as well as for the "positive orientations" of those responsible for their production; for the licensing of all printing presses and duplicating machines; for the state radio corporation; and for the direction of the youth and women's movements. In addition it ran the special campaigns of "public enlightenment" or "civic education" which were ordered from above at irregular intervals. (A campaign for cleanliness in public places, launched on a directive from the Heerser himself, was one of Serle's special preoccupations that year.) Constantly in competition with other cabinet offices for funds and influence, the ministry carried on an even more intense rivalry with the Propaganda Division of the Phalanx, which was an entirely independent operation. In general, the state and party bureaucracies were not only bigger than I could ever have imagined from the outside; they were also more complex and more incoherent, a machine whose parts flailed away endlessly at each other, while ostensibly working to the same end.

This was to prove useful to me later.

In addition to my other duties I was of course expected to supply Serle with all the gossip I could pick up about people in the ministry and outside it. In the basement of our building, next to the staff-canteen, there was a little room where the rabble of messengers, porters, bodyguards, drivers and suchlike, used to gather to drink coffee and smoke innumerable cigarettes. It was in this important meeting-place – with mops stuck into iron pails cluttering up the corners, and broken cupboards gaping open to reveal the emptiness within – that I learned most of the news I passed on to Serle.

Leave office . . . For obvious reasons I enjoyed Serle's public engagements most of all. I was never prouder of my position than when I stood on flag-bedecked platforms with him, or rode in procession in an open car. Never more alert, too. Reading rooftops and window-ledges, scrutinising waving hands and smiling faces, assessing times and distances, I had to be ready to respond to dangers before I had fully recognised them; to thwart the actions of those who might not even know until they had acted what their own intentions were.

From my very first day on the job I tried to acquire a special, professional view of death. By this I mean: I believed in it. It wasn't a remote improbability, a distant rumour, a suppressed fear. It was imminent. It was always lying in wait. It used all the chances given to it.

At the other extreme from our public outings were the evenings the Serles spent dining or playing cards with their friends. Sometimes, when they went out on private visits, Eva and I found ourselves the only people waiting in the street outside. That was how we became lovers. In dark suburban roads lined with overhanging trees and thick hedges, we entertained each other as best we could. On the front seat of the car. On the back seat. The floor. Facing this way. Facing that way. Maddened by the limited space we had to move in, we crammed ourselves into each other as if into receptacles smaller yet, never small enough for our passion. She could make the roof of my mouth tingle unendurably by caressing me elsewhere: a skill shared by no other woman I have known. After several months, however, without hard feelings, we decided that enough was enough. The risks were too great, the rewards too meagre.

Midnight . . . Eva dropped us at the door of the house, and drove back to the centre of the city, where she lived with her husband and children in a flat above a government garage: one of the perks of her job. I made the rounds, locking doors and windows, setting the alarms. I heard the Serles talking. Some nights, late, I heard him entering her bedroom. A door closed hollowly. Sleepless insects chirped just outside my window.

Days off were generally given to me at the weekend, when the Serles went to stay at the little country house, the Logie, which belonged to Mef. Serle and her brother. I spent most of my free time wandering on my own about the streets of Bailaburg, carried along by that imbecile sense of self-satisfaction known only to provincials who find themselves living in the metropolis. Here! At last! But I also remember certain moments during those wanderings – standing idle in the stone porch of a city church after the evening rush-hour; crossing a square and seeing an old man on a bench struggle to refold his newspaper, while the sun slid behind a cloud; watching two boys at a tram-stop amusing themselves by throwing their schoolbags at one another – I remember such moments for the very different quality of intensely expectant emptiness they had, their positively murderous wistfulness. I knew only too well whom I was hoping to meet; whose absence made my leisure appear empty; what I wanted to do with her when we did meet.

In the meantime I settled for the much humbler companionship of Edith. She was a tall, thin, gawky girl who worked as a waitress in a café into which I had dropped by chance one evening. Her walk alone told you almost everything you needed to know about her. Only someone artless and generous, you felt, would lift her pigeon-toed feet so high and put them down such a short distance ahead of her, covering so little ground with so much effort. Sitting at my table, talking to Edith, watching her hobble across the room to serve other customers, I sometimes wondered what it would be like to take another job, and settle down with her, and live happily ever after.

But ambition plagued me. My itch to beat the world. The thought of Gita Serle.

V

THAT WE MAKE one circuit only of the course our lives have to
run; that none of our memories is held "on approval", as shop-
keepers used to say, but has been bought forever, paid for irre-
vocably in breath and heartbeat – how hard that is for us to
accept! How we cling to the surreptitious hope or expectation that
another chance will somehow be given to us: that we will be
allowed in this world or the next to redeem all the errors we have
made, and use to advantage all the days and years we have wasted.
Such fantasies must always be preferable to the truth that the
past is as immutable as marble, as impalpable as a dream, and
equally terrible to contemplate in both aspects.

But I must proceed. I was writing about Gita. Her presence in
the house. Her presence in my mind. I think of her slender legs.
Then of the hollow of her cheeks. Then of her hands. Her skin.
(Imagine an olive ripening to the colour of a peach.) Her voice
was calmer and more assured than the movements of her eyes.

Of her past I knew only what gossip in the ministry and the
kitchen had told me. Her grandfather had died in a labour camp.
She had been working as a kindergarten teacher when she and
Serle had met. They had become engaged before his sudden
promotion. He was much older than her. She would have had a
title of some kind, if such "relics of feudalism" hadn't been
abolished by the Phalanx decades before.

But here I meet a problem I never anticipated when I set out on this task. Knowing at each stage all that happened to me subsequently, how can I really believe in my ignorance beforehand? How can I recreate that ignorance? When I look back it seems self-evident to me that I wanted to woo Gita from the moment Serle called me into his office and she made that idiotic remark to me about my duty and her body. (At the time I thought it devastatingly sophisticated; later I realised it was merely a kind of schoolgirl pertness and shyness that had made her blurt it out.) Yet I was so embarrassed when she said it, so young, so provincial, so anxious to please, so astonished to find myself in such company, I could hardly look at her.

That remained true for months after I'd joined her household.

Yes, I am sure it did. On the other hand, I can remember fairly early in my stay with the Serles solemnly perusing the story of my Old Testament namesake: the young man with the multi-coloured coat he had received from his father and the even more multi-coloured dreams of success he had made up for himself. I wanted to read again how that provincial prig and climber had been sold into bondage, into a great Egyptian household, and how he had succeeded in winning the devotion of his master's wife.

It was a comfort to me to remember the tale as I went round the living-room with a tray in my hand, helping Dirck serve drinks to the guests. I used to watch the sly, eager glances Serle's colleagues and superiors gave Gita, and relieve them of empty glasses they were busily rolling in the palms of their hands. (How they loved her for the title she didn't have, all those true democrats and sons of the Phalanx!) With that tray in my hand, what could I do to compel her to take notice of me?

But there were prior questions even more difficult to answer. Who was I to nurture such an ambition? Where had it come from?

It seems grotesque to say so, but it is the truth: what drew Gita and me together initially, and thus made possible all that followed between us, was our loyalty to Serle. Or at least our shared desire to think well of him. We tried hard: she because he was her husband, I because he was my boss and patron. (We were both new at our respective jobs.) We both failed. That drew us still closer together. Each knew that the other had failed. Each was determined to keep the knowledge from Serle himself. Thus we became allies.

Looks were enough to betray it. Pauses. Gestures. Inconsequential remarks. Sudden silences. Imperceptible steps. Indelible perceptions. Earnest retreats. Stealthy advances. None of them visible to any eyes but our own.

Things could have gone the other way. She could have hated me for seeing through her husband. For knowing that she saw through him, too. Instead, she drew comfort from my presence. She said so. At one stage there was a move in the ministry to have me chucked out. The two other deputy-ministers, Koch and Martinssen, who had been appointed after Serle, could not see why he should have a "special assistant" when they didn't. Serle fought hard for me. In the end an entirely predictable "compromise" was reached. They would all have special assistants. Gita welcomed the news. "I'm glad Josef is staying," she said to Serle. "I feel better when he's around." It was the first time she had spoken up for me in this way. To me, if not to Serle, it was obvious that it wasn't because of the danger from hypothetical assassins that she wanted me there. The inside of my throat contracted with pleasure. I couldn't have thanked her if I'd tried.

The truth is that it just wasn't in Gita's nature to hate you for understanding her. She wasn't like me, in that respect. (Maybe it was because she didn't hate herself.) I was so impressed with her sophistication, her aristocratic appearance and accent, that for a long time I couldn't see how simple-minded she was. Simple-minded and yet logical, too. Her marriage was evidence of both traits.

Her family had been much opposed to her marrying Serle. But one of the reasons she had been attracted to him, she was eventually to tell me, was precisely that he was a member of the Phalanx, like his father before him. And a member of the Guard too. They had met at a dance, at her college. "I was so sick and tired of the family talking about how badly we'd all been treated. I thought to myself, why shouldn't I try to make peace? Through him! Not just for my sake, but for everybody's. It seems so silly now. So pretentious –!"

Listening to her, I knew better how it was that we could be lying side by side as she spoke. Imagine having made such an effort . . . and to have ended up with Serle! After an error of that order, anything would be possible. Even me. By then she had transformed me, in my turn, into a personification of instinct, nature, the bleak, simple, truthful north and so on. Me! Such a solemn girl she was, for all her pertness and passion; such a grave, greedy face she had, and such a generalising, romantic mind . . . Actually, I was rather flattered by her portrait of me, at the time.

Her brother, Constantine, the young man I had seen with her on my very first visit to the ministry, helped too, in his way. Helped me, that is. He used to come to the house quite often. As time passed he made his contempt for his brother-in-law more and more obvious. "What is happening in the *inner councils* these days?" he'd ask Serle, and put his head to one side to show how attentively he was going to listen to the explanations and pronouncements that followed. "Go on! Amazing! Who'd believe it? Isn't it wonderful to get it all from the horse's mouth!" Flattered, Serle would continue to hold forth laboriously. Sometimes Connie brought friends with him, on these visits, and they would join in the fun. To Gita, who listened with her head lowered, they showed no mercy. In comparison with them I was a gentleman. Constantine's friends were tall, clean-complexioned young men rather like himself, and trousered girls who drawled and smoked cigarettes and put make-up on their faces in the middle of conversations. Horrible girls, whom I wanted to fuck and injure. Horrible young men. Horrible Connie 'S Koudenhoof. He used to call me "the watchdog", and snap his fingers at me and say, "Come here, boy, show your teeth, growl for the visitors" and so on. That was just one of his jokes. He pretended he was going to stab Serle with a butter-knife. He fired a cap-gun at my chest, at point-blank range. He drew me aside and asked me man to man what my price would be to shoot Serle and a few other members of the government.

50

"You mustn't take any notice of my brother," Gita said to me once, after some such incident. "He's always been a tease. He used to tease me like that when I was a little girl."

"I hate it."

"I'm sorry."

"I know you are. I wouldn't put up with it, otherwise."

Even now, writing down this conversation, and knowing what we were to become to each other, I am astonished at my boldness in talking to her like that. And at her – meekness, shall I call it? – in letting me do so.

Believe me: only that which a man dares to imagine ever becomes possible for him. It is the initial leap in the mind which is the hardest of all to take.

Another conversation. But first an introduction to it. I had been with the Serles for a year. The time had passed quickly. No one had ever threatened my boss's life and it seemed unlikely that anyone ever would. Politically things were quiet. The Centraad of the party had met, passed its resolutions, and dissolved. The Heerser, the Directorate, and the various cabinet offices had issued their respective reports showing the progress made on all fronts during the previous twelve months. Serle was kept very busy supervising the distribution of these reports, producing special versions of them for use in schools, editions of them in Braille for the blind, translations of them into the Kuni and Sedi tongues. Then we travelled about the country to attend the special thanksgiving rallies that were always held at that time of year. Gita stayed at home.

We appeared on many flag-bedecked platforms, while platoons of police and guardsmen held back crowds behind wooden barriers. Sometimes Serle took the salute as bands and floats and contingents from the Boys' Brigade and the Workers' Battalions and the Guilds of Sarmedan Women swung by; sometimes the parades were focused on figures of greater importance. Piet-Mack: First Secretary of the Directorate. Commis De Woudt: Minister of State Security. Judge Illuxst: Minister of Justice. Mef. Renier: Party Supervisor for Family Affairs. Autumn, more like the renewal of a promise than the end of one, showed itself in the stillness of the air, in the yellowness of the sun, in the deep, tense blue of the sky. The whole country seemed to lie in that trance-like state which so often precedes a great change. I wondered vaguely, without really knowing why I was moved to do so, what the impending change would be and where it would take place. Once I had to protect Serle from some over-enthusiastic schoolchildren, who were mobbing him for his autograph, of all things; once we were involved in what could have been a dangerous accident on the road, when I threw my body over his, as I'd been trained to do, the moment the car began to roll over after a nasty skid. Then it fell back safely on its wheels.

The tour over, we headed for home. Stepping through the front door of the house, I suddenly knew that the change I had been anticipating had indeed taken place – where I had least expected it. In me. In my feelings and state of mind.

I had simply had enough of Serle. Of pretending to admire and respect him. I could no longer make the effort. I would soon be as insolent towards him as Connie 'S Koudenhoof, unless we were separated or the connection between us was changed. I looked at Gita as she greeted him, extending her face to receive on her left cheek his homecoming kiss. It amazed me that she could bring herself to do it. Yet her eyes were upon me.

Serle was in high spirits. "A most successful trip. A wonderful response from the people. Couldn't have been better. They'll really be pleased up there." (A thumb jerking upwards.) "It's a pity those fools Koch and Martinssen will get more of the credit than they deserve – they always do. But it can't be helped." And more in the same vein.

Gita turned to me. "And you? Have you enjoyed your travels?"

"I'm not supposed to enjoy them."

We stood together in a sudden silence. "Well –" Serle gestured to the suitcase I had brought through the door.

I picked it up and carried it to his bedroom. Everything was in impeccable order. In my bedroom, too. I lay down on the bed, blank with the fatigue of travel and arrival; blank too with the realisation of how differently I now felt from when I had set out. Pictures of our travels returned haphazardly to my mind. Squares in provincial towns. Whitewashed villages hung about with bunting and pictures of the Heerser. Loudspeakers on poles. Serle returning to his seat with a flushed face and a queer wading moving of his arms, to the sound of well-drilled cheers. Faces.

There was a knock on the door. I stood up hastily, smoothing down my clothes. Gita entered. It was the first time, as far as I knew, that she had come to my room. Her face was intent: shyness and determination made it so. She closed the door behind her.

"What's the matter? You seem worried. Did something go wrong?"

"No – no –" I exclaimed in surprise.

Her irises moved in their oval whites, her lips flickered: enough to silence me.

Finally I said, "Nothing went wrong."

She turned as if to go. Then: "You'll stand by Trichardt, won't you?"

"I have no choice."

"Nor have I."

"Then we're agreed."

Simple, deceitful words. We had spoken of our understanding at last. But the alliance we had sealed in so doing was not one of loyalty to Serle. Far from it.

Later that night, when I met her in the hall of the house, I told her that I was going to ask Serle if I could be posted back to the Guard.

"Why? How can you? You just promised me you'd stay here –!"

"That's why."

"What do you mean?"

"Because," I said slowly, staring down at the polished, dully gleaming red bricks of the floor, and seeing as if they were incised into my mind the pale lines of mortar between them, "I want to keep the job for your sake, not for his."

I raised my eyes and looked straight into hers.

We stood a few paces apart from one another. Rung upon rung of illumined, motionless greenery was suspended in the air to one side of us. On the other side, the glass doors to the patio had been closed.

"So?" she said.

"So I think I better go."

She swallowed carefully. "Look, Josef, I'd like you to stay. But what you do doesn't matter all that much to me. Do you understand?"

"Yes."

"So?" she said again.

"So that's all the more reason for me to go."

She winced. It was the kind of reply she had wanted me to make, but did not wish to hear. Her lips parted. No sound came from them. We remained staring at one another before she turned and walked towards the door leading to the bedrooms. She was wearing a fawn cashmere cardigan slung loosely over her shoulders; its empty sleeves were dancing with agitation around her by the time she reached the door. She had to struggle with the handle to get it open.

Even then, after having made so explicit a declaration to her, I was once again overwhelmed by a sense of my own presumption. The boss's wife! One of the 'S Koudenhoofs! With looks like hers! Etcetera! I did not ask Serle to post me back to the Guard, but nor did I dare try to come close to her. I just hung fire for a day or two. From this paralysis I was rescued by Serle himself. With a mixture of embarrassment and doggedness, he asked me to spy on his wife. Well – er – not actually to spy on her – you know. More to – ahm – keep her under observation. As it were. And her brother too. I should report to him anything of – um – political significance I might overhear her say – er – perhaps when she didn't know that I was listening. In conversations with her brother, especially. Not that he suspected Mef. Serle of disloyalty, not at all, not for a moment, what an idea. But she was naturally close to her brother who was a – a – an irresponsible type. And she was – naive. Yes, that was the right word. She mightn't quite have grasped what her position involved. Or exposed her to. Or to what it exposed him, a deputy-minister, after all . . .

54

Embarrassed throughout, at this point he became quite incoherent. He stared at his desk. He got up from it and turned to his window, drawing aside the curtains to look at the raindrops that were sliding down the glass. Then he began rambling about the uncertainty of his own position, about his enemies within the ministry and outside it, about Brigadier Kerrick of the Command for the Preservation of Security and Order, about the attitude in certain circles of the Phalanx towards families like his wife's. Of course, when he'd got engaged to her he'd been an ordinary officer in the Guard. If he could have foreseen the course his career was going to take he might have – he would have . . . But the past was past. What was the point of speculating about might-have-beens? The fact was that his name was being associated with "a politically ineducable cell", composed of "dissolute aristocratic elements", who were plotting the "restoration of feudalism". (He uttered these phrases with a perfectly straight face.) Koch and Martinssen were behind it all, of course. Well, naturally, in the circumstances he had to take the most energetic steps . . . His career was at stake. More than his career: even his liberty, perhaps. I must keep my eyes and ears open. And if, heaven forbid, it emerged that his wife was involved in any questionable activities then he would have to . . . have to . . . cross that bridge when he came to it. He supposed.

I listened with a bowed head, an understanding mien, and a heart full of scorn and exultation. Yes, I understood. Of course, I would do whatever he wished. Naturally, I would be discreet. It went without saying that I had the greatest respect for Mef. Serle, and he could be sure I wouldn't do anything to cause her the slightest discomfort. But I'd watch her and her brother as closely as I could, and listen carefully to them, and report to him any conversations that might touch on the matters he had mentioned.

Then I withdrew to my little office down the corridor.

When Serle and I left the ministry after work that evening no sky was visible above the street-lamps: just a confined space in which bead-strings of rain swayed to and fro. The perfect autumn weather had broken the day after we had returned to

Bailaburg, and the rain had been coming down practically without pause ever since. The roads danced to its drumming. Windscreen-wipers on passing cars bowed and scraped like demented courtiers. Statues defied the downpour with their dripping swords and naked tits. Great black umbrellas bloomed suddenly in the door-ways of shops.

We entered the house to find Gita sitting with her brother and a young man who was not known to me. Gita got to her feet. Her face was tense. The rain was loud on the roof. I was sure Connie was going to make one of his insulting jokes or remarks; indeed, I wanted him to. But he thought better of it for some reason, and held his tongue. The two of them left shortly afterwards. I said to Gita, as casually as I could, "I didn't catch that young gentle-man's name." She told me what it was. So sweetly. So innocently. I wanted to laugh. Now that I was spying on her (on her hus-band's behalf!) I was not in the least afraid of her. I was her equal; indeed her superior; for the first time I was wholly sure that I could capture her. Who could stop me? Not she. Not now. Not Serle, either. Him least of all.

My biblical namesake gave me the idea of how I should pro-ceed. It was simple enough. I ignored her. No longer did I hang about hoping to meet her eyes and afraid of doing so. I spoke to her only when I had to, and then in the most insolently correct and indifferent manner. It was as if nothing had ever passed between us, or as if I considered our exchange to have been of no consequence. To Serle, lumbering about between us, quite un-conscious of the favour he had done me, I had never been more attentive and deferential, not even during my first weeks in his service. It seemed that he was my only care. Gita was puzzled, amused, irritated, hurt, roused, caught. I could see it all. I re-doubled my zeal towards Serle, my show of indifference to her

A week went by. A second. A third.

I will never forget the flat, uncanny weight and warmth of her hand, when she put it on mine for the first time. It was its burden of promise that made it so heavy; its burden of guilt that kept it so still.

56

VI

We were standing in the kitchen of the Logie. A house of softening shingles, smelling of damp. Surrounded by oaks and sycamores, whose leaves were beginning to fall. Once it had been the gatehouse to the 'S Koudenhoof estate. Now it was all that was left of the estate to Gita and Connie: the sole dowry she had brought to her marriage, her name apart.

No one else was in the house. It creaked nevertheless. The trees outside spoke together. We were shutting the place up for the winter. The water-tanks had been drained. The electricity had been disconnected. Storm-shutters had been put up over the windows of all the rooms, upstairs and down, except for the kitchen. The shadowed spaces around us made the kitchen appear both protected and threatened, secluded and exposed; light's last enclave. A cardboard carton stood on the table, in which Gita was packing various desultory items to take back to Bailaburg. A mincing-machine. A bottle of vinegar. It was to help them close the house that Serle had invited me to join them that weekend.

Our fingers did not cling together. They could not. My heart laboured in my breast, as if doing the work of hers as well as its own. The shadows from the hall crept closer. A noise like that of a sudden gust of wind reached our ears. Yet the leaves of the trees outside the window moved as delicately as before.

The sound we had heard was not the wind, but Serle returning.

He had gone to fill the car with petrol. Gita took her hand away. Tyres came to a crunching halt on the gravel outside.

"There," she whispered.

I picked up the box from the table, and took it outside to the little coupé. Serle was waiting at the wheel.

"Is there more to come?"

"Just a few things."

Gita came out of the house holding a spray of beech leaves. I went back to get the remaining set of storm-shutters. In the darkness of the basement, the asphyxiating blandness of many seasons' undisturbed dust in my nostrils, I opened my mouth wide to give a silent yell of exultation. There! The shutters rose in my hands like sheaves of paper; they seemed to fly of their own accord to the kitchen windows and stick there. No trouble. Nothing would be difficult for me hereafter.

Gita drove the car back to Bailaburg: a journey of about two hours. I sat in the dicky-seat outside. When I craned forward I could see her eyes and forehead in the rear-view mirror, and she could see me in it. We exchanged glances several times.

What colour should I call her eyes: green or brown?

In my memory they have the prominence and poignance of eyes in an Egyptian painting, staring solemnly yet childishly forward, even in profile.

Of Serle, on that drive, I remember particularly the small bald patch on the crown of his head, and the generous, almost lachrymose affection towards him that it roused in me. Also my obsession with the thought of how easy it would be for me to take out my gun and blow his skull into a hundred pieces.

I was paid to think about such things. He paid me.

That night Gita came into my bedroom. Late. Without switching on the light. She shivered and fumbled, whispered and hid her face, cried briefly and laughed even more briefly. Neither of us got much joy out of her visit. She was too afraid; I was too eager; she did not again make the journey from her bedroom to mine while Serle was in the house.

Thus there began a period of high passion and low farce. Our difficulty, mine and Gita's, can be summarised in a single, complicated question. How do you become the lover of the wife of a man whose bodyguard you are?

It's not so complicated, after all. I had to be with Serle all the time. When he was out of the house, I was out of the house. When he was at home with his wife, I was at home with his wife. I couldn't make love to her in front of him. My job prevented me from making love to her behind his back. Therefore, I couldn't make love to her.

I'd have given my life for Serle if a stranger had tried to attack him. At the same time his presence enraged me; so, rather more strangely, did his ignorance. He knew nothing of the despairing glances Gita and I exchanged; of the electric brushings together of our bodies we contrived as we passed through doorways; of the meetings of our fingers that took place beneath newspapers and bowls of fruit; of the words we whispered to one another at random moments – our names, simply, or "There!" which had become charged with a special meaning for both of us. These exchanges, and their accompanying gestures and drawn breaths, were as precious to us as they were dangerous, as eagerly awaited beforehand as they were exhaustively scanned in memory afterwards, as painfully burdened with desire as they were comically insufficient to express it.

We could not even speak to one another on the telephone. Not often, anyway. I was afraid of calling her from the ministry (someone might be listening at the switchboard); she was afraid that Dirck or Manuella, who always took the calls at the house, would recognise my voice even if I put a handkerchief over the speaker and tried to adopt a southern accent. Besides, when we did get through to each other, we had so little to say. "I love you." "Me too." "Do you really?" "I can't help it." "We're mad." "We'd be mad not to love each other." "I can't speak now." "Don't go . . . all right, if you must." "No."

The usual things.

I thought constantly of her: of her propinquity when I was away from her; of the distance between us when we were in the same room. Our awareness of the absurdity of our situation – its necessary, even professional absurdity, so to speak – actually helped to keep us going for a while. But every day of lavish promise and preposterous denial became more difficult to live through than the one that had preceded it. And the nights! They were endless. I would lie awake imagining over and over again that I heard her coming to see me; sometimes, far worse, that I heard Serle going to her room. "Get on with it!" I'd whisper like a lunatic to him, in the solitary darkness of my bedroom. "I want to sleep! I'm tired of waiting for you!" To escape from the house and its tiny night-sounds, each one of which seemed clamorous with meanings to my strained ears, rousing immoderate bouts of hope and breathless rage, I took to walking about the suburban streets for hours on end. It surprises me now that I was never picked up for questioning by the police during these nocturnal rambles. Only once, barefoot, in my pyjamas, did I make my way down the darkened passage of the house until I stood between the closed doors of the husband's bedroom and the wife's. With great care, like a man controlling the operation of a dangerous piece of machinery, I turned the handle of the door. It was locked.

Against me? Against Serle? How could I tell? I don't know for how long I stood there, the darkness around me less thick and baffling than that within my mind, before I turned and made my way back to my room.

All I wanted, or thought I wanted, was a week alone with Gita. Such a modest demand! How could we possibly be denied it? I won't repeat the various schemes I dreamed up in order to get that week alone with her. In the end, however, it was not with any particular hope of achieving my aim that I acted, but on an unpremeditated impulse. Overcome by rage at the waddle of Serle's backside just ahead of me, I tripped him as he was going down a flight of stairs in the ministry.

He plunged down the stairs with astonishing eagerness, like a diver, like a man hurling himself forward to meet his dearest friend, and landed heavily on the floor below: stunned, staring, bloodless. He had broken his collar-bone. He was taken to hospital and kept there for four days, to be treated for shock and bruises, as well as for the fracture.

So Gita and I had our honeymoon. It was briefer than I had wished it to be, but it was wholly ours nevertheless. Body to body, lip to lip, we found out what we liked best, most, unendurably. Then we made each other endure it again. And again.

From time to time, during those precious days and even more precious nights, I also took the opportunity to ask her questions about her life, her husband, and her brother and his friends

VII

A SINGLE LORRY waited at the level-crossing near the village, and a high-pitched warning-bell stung at the ear like the call of a cicada. I remembered the old man who used to close the gates at the crossing, and the smell of his hut. There he was: the same one! Home again. Or almost. The nearer we drew to the small cluster of trees and buildings ahead the slower our approach became. Brakes seemed to exert their pressure right inside my head and chest, and the train halted in an intense silence, shattered almost instantly by the reports of a few carriage-doors opening and slamming shut; my own among them. I descended on to the uncovered gravel platform. Beata came out of the little booking-hall.

She was wearing a grey, checked dress that came down almost to her ankles, and a much shorter coat that only just managed to meet across her protruding stomach. She must have been about five months gone. Even her face looked pregnant, somehow: it was broader, coarser, puffier, less expressive than I had remembered it. Yet she was still a peaky little creature. Hardly a woman.

She kissed me hurriedly. "Josef! Welcome home! It's been a long time!"

Her accent, the accent of home, rang strangely in my ears; almost as if she were affecting it for me. With a throaty roar from the engine up front, and a patient knock and sigh as each pair of wheels passed over a joint in the rails, the train began to move away. Nobody else seemed to have got off it: a few parcels had been dumped on the platform, that was all. On steps of different coaches the guard and conductor sailed by imperturbably, seeing and not seeing us, like all the other random objects they would pass on their journey. Copious sunlight fell from the bare, blue sky, but the air remained cold. Beata had put her arm through mine. We walked out of the station through an open gate at the end of the platform. An unpaved road, with a scatter of houses and small fields on both sides of it, ran towards the village square, several hundred metres away. There was nobody to be seen. The sparseness and emptiness of it all was amazing. Beata was talking busily about my mother, about my appearance, about some changes made in the shop. I hadn't said a word since my first greeting to her.

It was she who finally broke into the flow of her own remarks. She came to a halt in the middle of the road. "All right," she said, "you can ask me about the baby."

"Well?"

"It's Johann's."

"I thought it might be. Are you married to him?"

"You know I'm not."

"Are you going to marry him?"

"It doesn't look like it."

"Why not?"

"He doesn't want to marry me. He says he doesn't want to tie himself down."

"Oh! But he doesn't mind tying you down! Why didn't you write to me about it?"

"Because it's my business."

"And what does Mama say?"

Beata lifted her eyebrows upwards, then a moment later her eyes: a gesture I had forgotten and remembered again, instantly.

"What do you think? She carries on."

We were still in the middle of the road. A cart drawn by two horses was approaching, so I moved my little suitcase to the verge. Dry wintry grass stood up from the earth on both sides of a wire fence. The iron roof of the station blinked in the sun. There was nothing but sky beyond it.

"Well, I'll have to do something about it, won't I?"

"What?"

"Speak to bloody Fenter for a start."

Beata began to cry. "It's my business," she repeated.

"And mine. One whore in the family is enough, thank you very much."

She sniffed a few times before taking a handkerchief out of her coat pocket and blowing her nose. I picked up my suitcase. The cart went by, making a hundred different noises at once. Sand fell back on to the road from its iron-rimmed wheels. We resumed our walk to the village.

My mother was in good form. Characteristic form, anyway. "What do you think of your little sister?" she asked with a mad, sly coyness, seconds after I had stepped into the shop. "She's been a naughty girl, hasn't she? A naughty, naughty girl . . . Even before this I couldn't find a husband for her. Now –!"

Beata shook a fist at her, in rather fatigued fashion, and my mother grinned with delight to see it.

The home life of the Baisz family.

Difficult though it is for me to convey the depth of rage and depression which filled me from the moment I arrived in Vliss, I find it more difficult still to explain it. What did these people mean to me? Did I care so much about what happened to Beata? Why did coming back make me feel that all the changes I had brought about in my life, everything I had seen and done, even the famous places I had visited and famous people I had rubbed shoulders with – that all this had somehow been wiped out, made to appear of no consequence? I don't know the answer to these questions. All I know is the effect the place and the people had on me. I felt that I was trapped forever in the smallest and meanest aspects of my own life. The view from my bedroom over the square was exactly what it had been throughout my meaningless boyhood; the very sand out there seemed to know me; so did the breeze that stirred the net curtains for a moment, only to leave their folds hanging exactly as before, as they had always hung; a cricket in the back yard chirped brokenly, with the sound of a fingertip running along the teeth of a comb, stopping and starting again, forever. On the sill of the window halfway up the stairs there was a depression in the woodwork, with a knot standing up in the middle of it. Day after day, night after night, for years on end, I had touched it with my little finger as I passed up or down. I had called that touch "landing on the island". The sight of the depression and its knot, which I had quite forgotten about, the overpowering impulse I felt once again to land on the island, filled me with horror.

(And only now, as I write those words, do I think of another island, and the landings I was to make on it, in due course. A coincidence merely; a miserable coincidence. It rouses no horror; only weariness.)

Here I was; here was the family I came from; here was its history; I would never manage to make myself different from the rest – father miserably dead, mother crazy, one sister a whore, the other a betrayed girl, an object of sniggers and charity. And Josef, the big-shot, the son who had made good in the city! Who'd assaulted his boss and screwed his boss's wife! Who had then hastily taken leave from the situation he had created, with the boss now at home, still suffering from his injuries, and the wife proclaiming (in whispers) that they couldn't carry on as before, it was time for the truth to come out, whatever the cost . . .

What a triumph! When I thought of the pride with which I had looked forward to telling the people in Vliss about my life in the capital, and of the even greater pride I had taken in the thought of all I couldn't tell them, my self-contempt knew no bounds. One night, lying on the bed I had slept in as a boy, I actually smashed my fist down on my head several times. The pain made me feel no better.

I could have left it all behind. I could have caught the next train to Bailaburg and never come back. Instead I chose to involve myself deeper in Beata's life. In my mother's. In Fenter's. It is no mystery to me why I did it. Out of perversity, that's why. To feed my rage against them, and hence against myself; not to assuage it.

When I left Vliss, I did not go straight back to the capital, as I had originally planned to do. Instead I set out to search for Fenter. Beata did not know where he was, or so she claimed; she didn't even know if he was still in the Guard. I decided to begin by going to see his parents. I found his mother alone, in a small, neat house, full of over-stuffed furniture and little china objects on shelves. She was wearing black; her husband had died a couple of months previously. Mef. Fenter had her son's brows and eyes, and unhappy little jowls entirely of her own. When I told her my business, her jowls began to quiver. Then her mouth opened. She knew nothing about Beata's pregnancy. She was sure her son knew nothing about it either. He would have told her if he had. The girl had to blame someone. She had picked on him. Naturally she was trying to trap the best behaved and most promising boy she was ever likely to meet.

Seeing after some time that she wasn't going to change her line, I said quietly, "Mef. Fenter, do you know what I do?"

"No, I don't."

"Mef. Fenter, I'm a special assistant to the Deputy-Minister of National Guidance. I can help Johann a great deal – if I want to. I can also make things difficult for him, if I want to."

"A youngster like you?" she said scornfully. "Do you expect me to believe that?"

"You can suit yourself. Where is Johann now?"

"I don't see why I should tell you."

"I'll find out anyway. Through my office, if necessary. Goodbye, Mef. Fenter."

I was half-way down the short garden-path when she called out to me from the front porch of the house, her voice betraying some uncertainty for the first time. "He's stationed at Lockstendaal, at the sapphire mines."

"Thank you, Mef. Fenter."

An overnight train journey took me to Lockstendaal. Once

there I wandered for almost a whole day about the miles of camps and mine-workings scattered about in the woods before I found the company Fenter was in. Some of the men in it remembered me from basic training, or from the mountains, and gave me a big welcome. Only Fenter, who was now a corporal, looked downcast when he opened the door of the hut and saw me there.

Late in the afternoon, walking about among some trees near his quarters, we got the chance to speak to one another alone. Our conversation went off predictably enough. Moodily embarrassed on his side and stiffly distant on mine to begin with, and a little more cordial in the middle, it arrived eventually at a resentful agreement. He would marry Beata, even though "the last thing on earth" he wanted was a family to look after. In return I would use my "influence" to get him a job, preferably in Bailaburg, when his discharge from the Guard came through in a couple of months' time. He would write to Beata to tell her of the arrangement.

"And what if you don't get me a job?"

"That'll be tough luck on you. I'll do my best."

There was an awkward moment when neither of us knew whether we should shake hands on the deal. Fenter settled it by putting his hands in his pockets. He pressed the heel of his boot into the muddy ground and watched the mark he had made fill slowly with water.

"Well, you've got your way then, haven't you?" he said.

"Not really."

"Not really?" He looked angrily at me from under his wide brow. "What more do you want?"

"What I can't have. Another family altogether."

He treated the remark with the contemptuous silence it deserved, and turned back towards the hut.

On those eastern-facing slopes darkness came early. The wheels of the headgear above the mine-shafts ceased to spin. Black trunks of trees merged into the hillsides; then their branches merged into the sky. Floodlights shone over barbed-wire fences, and over double-tracks deeply rutted like miniature battlefields. The night

67

air breathed out damply. Howls and songs began to rise from the free workers' canteens. The prison-compounds were silent.

Fenter had fixed me up with a bed in his hut. I slept badly and woke before dawn. Rather than toss about uselessly on the narrow army cot, I got dressed and went outside. The sky was full of clouds, some of them torn open like paper to reveal areas of silver light within. Minute by minute, while I wandered among the trees, those areas of light grew brighter, their edges sharper; the surrounding clouds revealed more of their colour. At the perimeter-gate to one of the prison-camps some sentries were warming themselves round a brazier. They let me join them. Presently a couple of lorries crammed with prisoners and armed guards drew up at the gate. New arrivals. The prisoners sat in rows under tarpaulin covers. A few of them looked out at the place to which they had been brought; most were too weary or despondent to care. Their heads nodded incessantly to the rhythm of the idling motors. Counting began. Papers were examined by the light of headlamps. Some of the escorts took the chance to warm their hands at the fire. Looking up I caught the eye of one of the prisoners in the group nearest to me: a grey-haired man of indeterminate age, thinly clad, arms folded round his body in wretched, simian fashion. He was looking at me with a strange familiarity and lack of surprise, as if he had expected me to be there. I stared back at him. He did not move; only his head nodded, nodded, nodded to the rhythm of the engines, in a weary, affirmatory gesture. Then a telephone was banged down in the little wooden gatehouse. The escorts cursed and hurried back to their places. The gates opened for the lorries to pass between them. It was a relief to see them swallowed up indistinguishably among the huts and muddy roadways.

My business was finished; but several hours had to pass before I could take the train back to Bailaburg. A belated sun rose and contested feebly with the clouds about who the day should belong to. The clouds won. Rain began to fall. Sirens sounded. Groups of men carrying picks and shovels disappeared into the woods. Some of them had sacks pulled over their heads to shield

68

them from the rain. Coco-pans ran on narrow rails. Wheels inside the gaunt cages of the pit-headgear started to spin this way and that. I had fallen into a curious state of dissociation, of a kind which had possessed me occasionally during my childhood and only very rarely since then. I saw and heard everything that was happening around me, and took part in it; yet I was somehow removed even from my own infinitely diminished consciousness, let alone from all that was outside me. As in the past, I was the only one who knew this. I queued for breakfast with the others from the hut. I said goodbye to Fenter and shook his hand. I made my way back to Lockstendaal: a huddle of broken pavements, dingy shops, and neglected houses. On the station platform there was a kiosk which sold buns and two-day-old newspapers from Bailaburg. I bought one of the papers and sat down on a bench to read it.

A moment later I felt as if the bench beneath me had suddenly rocked and staggered, like a boat. My eye had fallen on a report, on the front page, about Deputy-Minister Serle. In an accident that had taken place three weeks before, the report said, the Deputy-Minister had sustained internal injuries, including a ruptured spleen, which had been unsuspected at the time. He had now been compelled to return to hospital. His condition was described as "serious".

A picture of Serle accompanied the report. It had been taken outdoors, on some public occasion. I could just make out my own blurred head among the others on the platform, at a little distance behind him.

VIII

IT WAS A long journey back to Bailaburg. The train panted through mountains, it waited endlessly past midnight at a junction called De Naauw, it hissed out steam at remote sidings where no one came or left. I did not sleep at all. My thoughts flew past me and returned: sometimes in the form of distinct words and images; more often hopelessly confused with the clamour and intermittent silences of the journey, with the changing postures of my body, even with the vaguely discerned shapes of mountains and plains passing outside.

It seems ludicrous to call those incoherent hours a period of stock-taking. Especially in view of the conclusions I came to. But within the limits of what I then believed about myself and was capable of feeling about others, I did look back and did try to look forward. To plan ahead. So far, I felt, I had acted instinctively, out of a conviction that perversity and boldness alone could compel the current of the world's energies to flow through me, instead of dispersing themselves at random around me; out of the conviction, too, that cunning and treachery enabled me to experience emotions I would otherwise never know. Love, for example. Tenderness. Glee. The results had been impressive. At least, until my return to Vliss I had thought them so. But for far too long, I now decided, I had allowed my domestic preoccupations to distract me from my career. Gita, in short. But her position was quite different from mine. She could afford to do whatever she liked. She was a 'S Koudenhoof on the way down. I had to be more careful. I was a Baisz, rising.

Look what I had done to Serle! Who in Bailaburg was in the least interested in me, besides Serle? If I had managed to find another patron, someone else to guard, then I could have forgiven myself for having thrown the last one downstairs. But I had never looked for another boss. It hadn't even occurred to me to do so. The absurd, humiliating truth, which I had failed to recognise, was that because of Gita I had actually tied myself much more closely to Serle than I might otherwise have done. To the very end. With that attack on him I might have finished off both of us. Why had I done it? There was only one answer: the image of Gita's face with its heart-shaking smoothness and intentness as she concentrated upon her pleasures. That was why. She was to blame. It was her fault that I had remained wholly dependent on the favour of Serle; her fault that he now lay in hospital, suffering from horrible, irrelevant injuries. Another victim, like myself.

Towards noon the city began to accumulate itself on both sides of the line: suburbs and factories; spires and subways; cobbled streets with tram-tracks running through them like silver veins; at last the echoing vault of the central railway station. My leave was over. It is no exaggeration to say that by the time the train came to a halt I positively hated Gita. I felt about her almost as if she were a member of my own family, dragging me down. Bitch! Whore! Upper-class cow! It amazed me that I had had to go all the way home, and then chase after Fenter to those hideous mines, and then read in the paper about Serle's condition, before I could realise how trivial was my obsession with her and how great was the harm it had done me.

But no more. Now I knew. Her time was up.

I bought a paper at a news-stand to see if there had been any further reports on Serle's condition. Nothing. I threw the paper into a waste-basket. Light fell through high, clerestory-like windows into the main concourse of the station. People went

71

about their business in a leisurely, noontide manner. A loud-speaker boomed and whispered its announcements, with a chime before each one. Everything was peaceful, except for the secret beating of my heart. From a phone-booth on the concourse I called the office of Brigadier Kerrick of the Command for the Preservation of Security and Order. (I had taken his number out of Serle's private directory months before.) A secretary answered. I told her who I was and said that I had some information to pass on to the brigadier. To my gratification, and a little to my surprise, she gave me an early appointment with him.

I spent the night with poor, hobbling Edith, from the café, whom I had continued to see from time to time over the last few months. She lived in a flat with her aged mother, who was turned out of the biggest bed in the place whenever I called; and with a younger brother, also in the catering trade, who resented my visits. (The mother was past having articulate views on any subject.) Edith and I spent the evening sitting hand in hand in a cinema; then we went to a restaurant on Signal Hill for a sausage and a glass of beer. The bars were open, music came out of basements and back-rooms, men sold peanuts and hot corn-on-the-cob from steaming barrows. It was a pleasure to be back in the bustle and indifference of the city, despite all I had on my mind. A short tram-ride took us back to the flat and its double bed. Edith was usually awkward and timid, but she sometimes went in for fits of childish high spirits which had always appealed to me. That night her trick was to pretend to be an octopus, of all things, with tendrils waving, eyes staring, and a tiny triangular mouth. The mouth gave her a great deal of trouble. But she got it right in the end. And put it in the right places.

The next morning I set out in search of the address that had been given by Kerrick's secretary. It turned out to be a non-descript office block in a rundown area on the other side of the city. The building had no nameplate outside: just a plain gold number painted on the fanlight above the main entrance. No uniforms were to be seen anywhere. The people inside it betrayed their profession only by the look of bored brutality on their faces.

And by something more difficult to describe. A kind of arrogant furtiveness in the way they looked at you.

Brigadier Kerrick, however, was quite different in appearance not only from his henchmen, but also from my preconception of what one of the much-dreaded bosses of the Compresecor would be like. I was to learn later that he prided himself on his "normality". "Ordinary" was another word he used fondly about himself. Small, bald, and jocular, he wore a casual sports-jacket and a pair of rather flashy, plum-coloured trousers which were held up by a striped belt around a comfortable belly. There was a variety of brown marks and speckles on his scalp; his eyes, behind boyish, horn-rimmed spectacles, were a twinkling blue; his moist lips hung open. He looked "American", I remember thinking, though I really had no idea what Americans looked like. To indicate agreement he jerked his head forward; when he laughed he threw both hands into the air and uttered a single, convulsive bark.

Our conversation was a grave one, about a grave matter. But all the same I made him laugh a couple of times. The first time was when I told him that Mef. Serle and I were "more than friends".

"You mean, you –?" His hands were clasped on the desk in front of him, and he gestured towards me with his thumbs. I nodded. "And she –?" He repeated the gesture, and I nodded again. "Well I'm damned!" he exclaimed, leaning back in his chair. Then he laughed. The sound was almost like a sneeze, and so was the convulsion of his body that accompanied it. For some time he sat in silence, looking at me. Twinkling at me.

I explained that after the deputy-minister had gone into hospital, we had been alone in the house together for a few days. It was then that we had – well . . . and that she had told me . . . what I wished to tell him. (Pillow-talk. Gita's confidences. The one substantial item of information that my weeks of spying on her and 'S Koudenhoof had produced.) Connie 'S Koudenhoof, I now repeated to Kerrick, was a member of a secret group called the Silver Fern. It took its name from a bush that grew on the slopes of the Maaibergen, not far from the city. The people who belonged to it went there several times a year. Each of them plucked a frond of the plant, on which they renewed their oath of allegiance to one another and to the "old order". They also carried out "exercises": of what kind I did not know. Several of the people in the group had been Connie's friends since his schooldays. Some of them – and I gave their names – had visited the house with him.

"And Mef. Serle? The lady herself? Is she a member?"

"If I thought so, I wouldn't have come here."

Kerrick's eyes contracted, his chest heaved, he uttered the convulsive sound of his mirth. "I understand. A man of honour!"

I looked modestly at the floor.

"Has she told the deputy-minister about it?"

"No. She said she was afraid to."

"Have you?"

"No. How could I? Even if he wasn't so ill, I mean –"

Kerrick pinched his gaping nostrils between thumb and fore-finger, then rubbed them roughly with the back of his finger alone. "Yes, in the circumstances it would be difficult. So what brings you to me? How did you know of me?"

"The deputy-minister once mentioned your name in connection with this kind of work."

There were no further questions for the moment. In a rumina-tive, almost absent-minded tone of voice Kerrick said, "We know quite a lot about the Silver Fern, actually. We've been watching them for some time. It's not a group we take too seriously. You know what those people are like. Literature. Hysteria. Self-importance. When the time is ripe we'll do whatever's necessary. As for young 'S Koudenhoof –" I thought he was going to laugh again, but he suppressed it. "We certainly know about him. All about him. Don't look so disappointed . . . It's very patriotic of you to have come and told me the story." Without a pause, without even a change of expression, he went on. "What do you really want out of this, Baisz? Money? Is that why you came?"

I answered him directly. "No sir. Work."

"Oh." And again, "Oh." He scratched his freckled scalp through the few strands of sandy hair growing from it. "What sort of work?"

"The same, I suppose. Only for someone else. It's what I'm trained for."

He asked me a few more questions. I told him that if I did not get another job I presumed I would simply have to return to the Guard; that I had graduated from Burzenack; that I'd received a special commendation from my O.C. at Kazerne for saving Serle's life. He listened attentively and made a couple of notes of what I had said. Finally, getting to his feet and putting his hands on the small of his back as he straightened himself, like a man suffering from rheumatism or some such ailment, he said he would see what he could do.

That rheumatic gesture made him seem slightly more reliable, or at any rate well-disposed to me: heaven knows why.

But to tell the truth I didn't care all that much, for the moment, about what he had made of me. In my breast there was a bubble of serene self-assurance which made me almost indifferent to the consequences of what I had just done. The action itself was its reward. That feeling of absolution and renewal it produced; the conviction of being in command of my own life once again – there was nothing like it!

Now: back to the house. To confront Gita. She could do nothing to me. I had passed beyond her reach.

The front door opened. Dirck greeted me sombrely and led me into the drawing-room. Gita was sitting in an armchair next to an open fire. She looked up when I came in. The flames sent their ever-changing patterns over those of the chintz and glass in the room.

"You," she said. Then, "Thank you, Dirck."

He withdrew. I remained standing in the middle of the room. We had parted with hands outstretched to one another: now metres of empty space lay between us. She asked if I had heard what had happened to Serle. I enquired about his condition. She stared into the fire. Each of us, perhaps, waited for the other to break. Neither of us did. It was impossible, just a moment later, to imagine that either of us ever would.

The period that followed was in some ways one of the strangest of my life. It was so dull. So pointless. Serle remained in hospital, making slow progress. Gita and I barely spoke to one another. She appeared to find my presence as burdensome as I found hers. I kept out of her way, spending much of my time at the ministry, where I pretended I had various odd jobs to do. During that time I used Serle's name to fix up Fenter with a job on a newspaper in Boschoff. A single phone-call did it, followed by a single, illegibly signed letter on Serle's notepaper. For the rest I drank much government tea, and listened inattentively to much bureaucratic gossip.

Every day Gita went to the hospital and stayed there for hours on end. With its domed wings and arched entrance the hospital looked rather like a place of worship: I imagined her doing penance inside it, trying to expiate her guilt for having betrayed her husband and for having made light of his injuries. I was not invited to accompany her on these visits. Only after Serle, at his own request, had been relieved of his duties in the administration "for an indefinite period", did Gita tell me that he had been asking to see me.

"When can I go?"

"Now."

He lay on his back, under a white counterpane. His skin was smooth and pale; a few new lines were deeply incised into it. He needed a haircut. But he was less changed than I had feared. It was a relief to be in one room with him, after having anticipated the meeting for so long. The moment I walked in I could see that he could do me no harm; he had no accusations to make against me.

His eyes shone more brightly than ever before. They seemed positively blinded by the gleam upon them. Every time he blinked I thought he was at last going to speak. Gita sat at his side. There were flowers on a cabinet next to his bed, and some books and papers. The glitter in his eyes grew brighter and brighter; it was suddenly transformed into two drops which shivered, toppled

76

over, and ran down his cheeks. In a remote voice, speaking between long, blank pauses or absences, his hands touching at one another above the counterpane, he told me what I had already heard from Gita. He was giving up his job. He didn't know if he would ever be able to take it up again. Or if they would want him. He would never be the same man again. He knew it. The doctors knew it. It was his duty to go.

Gita leaned over and wiped the tears from his cheeks, like a devoted wife. Her lips moved, but she did not say anything.

"You must find another berth, Josef. Or go back to the Guard." He made an attempt to smile. "You can't give me the help I need. Not any more. I never thought it would all end in this way. A stupid accident, a moment's carelessness – and now this!"

His eyes closed. He was too tired to listen to my expostulations and reassurances. Gita gestured me to be silent. We remained looking at each other. The skin round her eyes was shallower, somehow, than it had been. Poorer. Plainer. I nodded and left the room. My shoes squeaked on the shining linoleum of the corridor. I had almost reached the entrance when Gita caught up with me. To my surprise she said, with some effort, "I want to talk to you. Let's go for a walk."

She dismissed Eva, who had brought us there in the car, and we went to a park nearby. A sweet cold mist hung in the air, drawing a distinctive scent from everything it silvered with its drops: mouldering leaves, branches of trees, painted metal. Lawns and avenues were empty save for a few reluctant nursemaids with their well-wrapped charges, and an occasional uniformed keeper. Distance transmuted the noise of traffic into a melancholy sigh or hiss, interrupted from time to time by brief wails. We walked between clipped beech-hedges that held their own dead leaves fast in the mesh of their branches. At intervals this alleyway opened out into circular, apse-like spaces, where statues and metal benches faced one another. I wiped the moisture off one of the benches with my handkerchief, but we sat on it for only a moment; it was too cold. Then we stood on a bridge over an ornamental pool.

It was only when we were leaning side by side over the balustraded parapet of the little bridge that Gita spoke. Looking down she asked, simply enough, "What are we going to do?" Then she said, "I feel like a criminal."

She was going to say more, but I interrupted her. "You feel like a criminal? What about me?"

She gestured sideways towards me with her shoulder and elbow, without turning her head: a consoling, familiar movement. "I know. I understand." Mournfully, still staring at the water, which seemed to shine with an impure light from within rather than to reflect anything from the dull sky, she added, "But you're not his wife."

"No." The back of my neck burned with pleasure and fear. Irresistible sweetness ran through my veins. I felt weak, as if undone by desire. "And you're not the one who pushed him downstairs."

I thought at first that she had not heard me. She was still leaning over the parapet, looking down at the water. Then I saw that her body was bowing lower and lower, as if weights she could not bear were being put one by one on her shoulders. I added another, perhaps the heaviest of all.

"I did it for you."

Her face sank into her trembling hands.

Minutes passed; or what felt like minutes. Her face remained hidden from me. She was wearing a little fur hat: black and silver. The look of it from behind made me feel that I was talking to an animal. I said again, "I did it for you."

She did not move. I raised my voice. "Look what I've thrown away for your sake! My job, my boss, my career, my self-respect – everything! For you! And what about him? He's finished! Broken! He's the only innocent one, and he's the one who's suffering most. I hope you're proud of yourself!"

And more in the same vein.

She turned and ran towards a wooden shelter some distance away. There was a small smear of mud on the calf of one of her boots, at the back. The sight moved me more than anything else about her. Moved me to pursue her. To hold on. Not to relent.

I found her crouching on a bench in the corner of the hut. Her face was contracted; her eyes enlarged. I stood over her and shouted, "Now go and tell him! Go on! That's all he needs, in the state he's in! Tell him what I did, and why I did it!"

"I never asked you to," she said faintly, like a child. It surprised me that she could speak at all.

"But you took advantage of it. Didn't you?" With the side of my clenched fist I hit the wooden wall of the hut as hard as I could, just above her head. "Didn't you?"

"Yes, I did. I did."

I turned and walked away. The sound of her sobs did not carry far. At the main road I caught a tram, which dropped me near the house. I packed my bags and gave Dirck the name of the café Edith worked in, so that he could pass on any messages for me. Gita had not yet returned by the time I left.

IX

To use the insidious form of untruth known as "hindsight" in order to re-create the untruth of bygone ignorance: that, I now see, is the real art of the autobiographer.

What a job!

Sometimes it seems to me even more ambiguous than any other task I have ever taken on. Which is quite a claim to make, all things considered. Told one way, looking forward as it were, and proceeding from one event to the next, my story may seem to be a mere sequence, without design or purpose. Told another way, looking backwards, it can be made to resemble a plot, a plan, a cunningly involuted development leading to a necessary conclusion. Being both narrator and subject, how am I to know which way to look?

Besides, I have to contend like everybody else with the idiotic haphazardness of memory. While crucial moments of my life, as I believe them to be, have become blurred and doubtful in my mind, other moments to which I can attach no importance at all will suddenly reappear before me with a matchless immediacy. One might almost imagine that such moments have been preserved in their pristine state precisely by their inconsequence; or even by the fact that they had apparently been forgotten.

But whatever way the story is told, whether as a plot or a series of accidents, as a design or a mere addition of day upon day and year upon year, it must lead eventually to this moment. Here. Now. To me sitting in this chair and putting these words to paper, while the sun begins to set behind the mountains, and indigo, veil-like shadows hang from its upward-pointing rays or rods, as if they are part of some celestial backdrop, suitable for a grand pageant of gods and giants.

No such creatures appear, however. The villagers talk to one another through the dusk; footfalls sound on unmade roads; cows low and dogs bark; lamps appear at windows; and Josef Baisz goes out for his evening stroll, accompanied by his ever-faithful body-guard. Bit by bit the stage-set in the west is dismantled. The theatre is plunged into darkness. I take a frugal dinner and return to my desk. To my task. To spewing forth my deeds and mis-deeds. Time is short. The days and nights pass quickly. Just as I once shivered and swooned with a quasi-sexual delight as I announced to the bent head and bowed shoulders of Gita Serle what I had done to her husband, so my hands now tremble with excitement as I slip into the typewriter, at the beginning of each new page, as many sheets of paper and carbon as I can cram between roller and carriage. One for the Heerser, one for Max Spass, one for my wife, one for Beata (who will never receive it), one for Gita, one for my stepson . . .

Greetings to you all. Never fear, I am not going to apostrophise you at length. I am returning this very moment to that other Josef Baisz, my predecessor in the role: the one who left the Serles without ever imagining that the time would come when he would settle down in front of a typewriter to write about . . . leaving the Serles! What is to become of him now? What further adventures await our dauntless hero as he makes his way towards us through the long avenues of time?

Well, the modest truth is that he proceeded to hold a succession of commonplace jobs on the fringes of the government service. He became a petty functionary, or even less than that.

But he did not repine. Believe me, I know. I remember.

Mostly I continued to live in Bailaburg; but I also spent periods in Welgelegen, the second city of the southern provinces;

in Port Margriet; and back in the north, in Boschoff. I worked for a spell as one of the pool of drivers in the Ministry of the Interior; then as one of the ministry's internal security officers; then as a bodyguard once again. I guarded in turn the chief of a major state investment corporation (brewing, petrol, paper, bicycles); the State Actuaris; and a high official in the central bureau of the Phalanx, Ernst Deen by name, who claimed he had received many threatening letters and phone-calls from unnamed enemies. It turned out that Deen was in fact suffering from delusions; my handling of him, when he finally and publicly went off his head during an official visit to Port Margriet, so impressed the Prefect of that city that he approached me and asked me to become one of his aides. This was a substantial promotion, the biggest that had come my way since Serle had first summoned me to Bailaburg. I was elevated from the rank of N.C.O., so to speak, to that of subaltern. My appointment in Port Margriet lasted for almost a year; at the end of it, however, as I shall relate in due course, I blotted my copybook over "the Watermaier affair", and was sent back to Bailaburg in disgrace.

Dear friends and readers, I have just summarised months and years. Fair enough. They had gone by almost unnoticed, somehow. I had grown older; I had learned more about the world and the people in it; I had come to understand better the nature of our political system – of which more presently. One unexpected consequence of all this was that I had become much more tolerant (in retrospect) of my own family and of the village of Vliss than I had ever been before. I had realised that almost everything that had seemed to me shameful and singular about my family had its parallel in the lives of others; that it was perfectly possible to emerge from the homes of the rich and powerful with much the same feeling of rage and distaste as I had emerged from mine. An obvious conclusion, it now seems; but then it had a greatly liberating effect on me. It had even occurred to me that to produce such feelings was one of the functions of the family, as an institution. Mine had done it after its fashion; others did it in theirs. I no longer felt like writhing inwardly when I thought of my mother's eccentricities, or of the conversations I used to overhear on the village square, or of the excitement Beata and I would feel over some wretched function in the church-hall. Even the little school I had attended now seemed to me to have been a far better training-ground for life in the metropolis than I could ever have guessed it would be.

How swiftly, for example, the word used to spread through the schoolyard that so-and-so was in trouble with the bully of the school; how pale the offender went when he realised what was in store for him; how vainly he looked for a response from the rest of us to his sick, ingratiating smile; how sorry we felt for him, and how glad that it was his turn to cop it and not ours; with what terror and zeal everyone would join in the last mad pursuit and capture, once the signal was given.

I saw it many times: in marble-floored palaces, in dusty offices packed with filing-cabinets and ink-spattered desks, in summer resorts above the Great Lecke Lake, where our masters had their country cottages.

Yet the Phalanx, which ruled so decisively over so many aspects of our lives, was no longer the murderous, self-consuming body it had been a couple of decades earlier. Officials, even high officials, who were disgraced or fell into disfavour were very seldom shot; many of them escaped imprisonment; some were allowed to begin new lives almost immediately as railway porters and gas-meter readers. The position of the party within the country, however, remained unassailable. It controlled all our major industries; the machinery of state was subordinate to it; church and army, schools and newspapers, were its organs; all avenues of advancement ran through it. Within the apparatus there were of course various factions or fiefdoms, each with its own head and its special areas of power; these formed allegiances and enmities in a continually shifting pattern, which owed something to differences over policy and more to differences of personality. When a feudal overlord grew too mighty, or too independent, he was cut down; then all those who served him were involved in his ruin. This was clearly understood by all.

From my point of vantage, however, it sometimes seemed to me that the convulsions which took place within the hierarchy sprang as much from a deep-seated desire on the part of the very highest authorities to entertain the masses, as from any real threat to their power. To see the bosses tumble and the mighty ones tremble; to know that so-and-so's turn had come at last, after all the cheers and high living, made up for a lot of humiliation and deprivation out there; it helped greatly to reconcile the mass of people to their powerless and humdrum existence.

But not me. Not Josef Baisz. I had no intention of remaining a member of that mass. Whatever my fate might be, I was determined it was not going to be humdrum. Therefore, as just one of the necessary steps I had to take on my way upwards, I became a member of the Phalanx. The Prefect himself swore me in, while I was working in Port Margriet, with the grave, proud, compassionate air of a priest admitting another to his holy fraternity. It would be too simple to say that I joined precisely because I knew the Phalanx to be riddled with lies and corruption – though it was. Or that I was deliberately attaching myself to the state-power which had employed and then destroyed my father – though it had. Or that I was ambitious for status and worldly advancement – though I was. There was something even more important at stake in all this, for me. More sinister too.

How can I put it? I was not ambitious merely for money or power or fame. My ambition was both grander and more private. It was to be – myself. Or what I felt I might become. To be wholly and thoroughly what only Josef Baisz could be. I was still bemused, in other words, by the idea of proving myself to be a man of special talent, even perhaps of genius; the possessor of an insidious, unfathomable gift, whose true nature I had only just begun to perceive. What a responsibility! What an opportunity! My honour as well as my fate were at stake. I owed it to myself not to flinch. And – no less – I owed it to the world at large. No second chance would be given to either of us, in the eternity behind and ahead, when there had been and would be no Josef Baisz.

84

I couldn't have articulated all of this at the time. No matter. One thing I did know was that I could find no more suitable or worthy framework for my activities than that offered by the state and party. When, much later, I took a job for a while with a private person – with the film-actress, Dafne Mainckies – I felt it as a definite derogation of my dignity. The underworld made no appeal either. I wanted the best that was going. Only the government of the Republic could provide that. Just as it was. And as I was.

You see the catch? How easy it always is, with somebody else's life; or even just with the benefit of hindsight! Yes, I believed that I was the owner or master of my gift, of my malign talent. It never occurred to me that I was choosing to become its possession or servant. That it would be able to anticipate every thought and move I made, to use me and trick me and outwit me, until it would finally bring me here. But even now, when I know what remains to be done, once the misery and excitement of this narrative is behind me, I would merely be making a bow in the direction of conventional morality if I were to declare that I have spent my life serving the principle of denial, of negation, of de-creation. The very opposite is true. The master I have served, the one who hides in the grooves of my nerves, who runs in my blood, who uses my eyes to look at the world, is the presence within me of the spirit of life itself; of that impulsive, aboriginal folding-back of matter upon itself from which all consciousness has sprung.

That's why there is only one way to deal with him.

X

I HAVE RUN far ahead of my story. Let me go back to my days as a petty functionary. All the opportunities and experiences that came my way during this period I owed to Brigadier Kerrick. He had indeed stepped in, as I had hoped, to prevent me being sent back to the Guard, after my departure from the Serles. In return for this favour I was of course expected to give information to the Compresecor about the people I drove around, or guarded, or simply had the chance of observing. My contact throughout was an agent called Trager, whom I used to meet at irregular intervals in the Crescent Café, on Stann Road, near the centre of Bailaburg.

I always found him waiting for me, crammed into the same booth at the back of the café, with a glass of brandy and a cup of coffee in front of him. Their mingled fumes came in wafts towards me, as he asked his questions and solemnly wrote down my answers in a little notebook. Small, fleshy ears clung like naked cherubs to the sides of his shaven skull. Occasionally he opened his mouth in an unconvincing grin, revealing the broken ivory inside. He was a great admirer of Kerrick, and was as jealous of his favour as a dog of its master's. At our very first meeting I had learned that Kerrick was "keeping an eye on me", and that if it hadn't been for him I'd have been sent back to whatever goddam place I came from. Hardly a meeting went by subsequently without Trager solemnly warning me not to "try any tricks". Kerrick would find out if I did, and then he would nail me. Trager's feebly suspicious eyes, which usually floated half-closed in their pouches of fat, widened with wonder when he spoke of the shrewdness and sagacity of his boss. He was so clever, he said, he could have been a professor. And persistent! Once he got his teeth into people, they were goners. With a wagging finger he spelled out the word for me. G-O-N-E-R-S.

The walls of the Crescent were a glossy, greasy yellow, all dirt and shine; only in such cafés does one see such walls. The waiter was a homosexual youth whom Trager called "Darling" with a meaningful smirk at me every time. The proprietor knew, I was sure, what Trager's job was and hence why we met.

I didn't care. The arrangements were not my responsibility. I did not try any tricks. I answered the questions put to me, but refrained from volunteering information on topics which Trager did not raise. I had decided, looking back on my interview with Kerrick, that it could be dangerous to appear too eager in one's approaches to the Compresecor. Nor did I ever complain about the smallness of the sums which Trager reluctantly passed across to me at the end of every session. His eyes shone with a distant, reflective gleam, like a man looking into a fire, as the envelope containing the money disappeared into my pocket.

I can't say that Trager ever really relaxed in my presence; that would give the wrong impression. But there were occasions, after our business was concluded, when he ordered another brandy, fixed his muddy eye on me, and proceeded to tell me about his domestic woes. These chiefly featured his little girl. She was backward. You know – up here. (Pointing.) Where was the justice in it? She was all right now, she was small. But what would happen later? When she grew up? There were all sorts of people who would take advantage of her. Boys. Unscrupulous bastards. He blinked slowly at the thought, and the corners of his mouth turned further down than usual, making their way through the pale wedge of flesh that served him for a chin.

But he rebuffed me smartly whenever I tried to advance on

such intimacies and get him to talk about the boss he hero-worshipped. All I received then were slow head-shakings. Expulsions of brandy-laden breath. Instructions to mind my own business.

So I never did find out whether Kerrick was married, or where he lived, or what his habits were, or how he had entered the Compresecor. He remained for me, until the very last time I saw him, entirely a creature of his office, of his position; a purely professional man. On that last occasion, however, the intensity of his fear, surprise, and embarrassment transformed him, paradoxically enough, into something resembling a clockwork toy or marionette.

What a strange medium time is: transparent when you look back, when it is of no use to you to be able to see through it; utterly opaque when you try to look forward.

In one case only do I know how the information I passed on to Trager was used. Some months after I had left the service of that investment chief I mentioned a little while ago, the then Minister for State Enterprises was involved in a scandal which led to his downfall. In newspaper reports of the "nefarious conspiracy" he was supposed to have organised I found references to various meetings at my man's house, about which I remembered telling Trager. Many months later, again, I bought a lottery ticket from my former boss, at a booth in Falckenhaim Parade. I recognised him, sad and bearded though he now was, before he recognised me. When our eyes met I saw in them not only shame but also deep reproach. Thereafter I always made a point of buying my lottery tickets from him. We even took to drinking a glass of beer together, each time. He would put up the shutters on his booth and go with me to an open-air café nearby. Then he would scratch about in his brand-new whiskers and tell me that he had really deserved better treatment from me. I never defended myself. I bought him another beer. He drank it.

But now – as promised – an account of "the Watermaier affair". That is, my guardianship over the dead body of the world-renowned scholar and trouble-maker, Professor Hans Watermaier: a mission that began in embarrassment and ended in farcical humiliation and disgrace.

It happened, as I have said, when I was working for the Prefect of Port Margriet. On the evening of Watermaier's death the Prefect began receiving reports that a group of students were planning to snatch the body in order to stage a "political" funeral. One can imagine the kind of thing they had in mind: flags, torches, tears, speeches, clenched fists, mischief. To forestall them I was sent out post-haste to the village in which the professor had been living with his sister, during the years of his enforced retirement. The body still lay in their cottage. My instructions were simply to make sure that nothing was done to it before it had been stowed safely underground.

So off I went. The village was about two hours' drive into the hills. It turned out to be much like the others I had passed on my way up: hardly more than a few stone and iron buildings in a group, and a scatter of habitations recessed into the thinly wooded slopes all round. Small fields had been cleared on both sides of the road for cows and goats to graze on, uphill and down; and there were also some terraces of apple-trees, sustained by a kind of basket-work peculiar to the region. Somewhere out of sight a stream kept up a ceaseless conversation, interrupting its own discourse from time to time with clear, irrational little chuckles. I had set out before dawn; now the early morning sunshine sent long shadows into every corner. At the police station (where they had been warned of my arrival and told not to interfere unless I called for their assistance) I was directed to the Watermaier cottage, about a kilometre distant. The air seemed to hold motionless the scents and random sounds of every other autumn morning I had known. On the horizon, rising above many rounded hilltops, towered the purple peak of the Enckelberg.

Mej. Watermaier, sister and sole heir of the deceased, met me in front of the house. She greeted me noiselessly, with a solemn nod of the head, befitting her status as chief mourner and mine as bearer of the regime's condolences. But beneath half-closed, flimsy eyelids her gaze was full of the mingled panic and embar-

89

rassment of grief. I said the usual words and handed her the letter I had brought with me.

It made no mention, I knew, of the real reason for my presence. It introduced me as the Prefect's "personal representative", with instructions to be helpful "in any way possible" at this time of "private and national bereavement". Then it went into practical details. A hearse was following me, and would arrive at some time in the afternoon; the body of her brother would be taken to the city, and would lie for a day in the Klainsaal of the Prefectuur; a modest official funeral would follow the day after. "Thus," the letter concluded with a flourish, "in a spirit of reconciliation we will unite to do honour to one who was such a greatly gifted, if sometimes such a greatly errant, son of the Republic. Yours in sympathy . . ." Every word of it had been cleared on the highest level in Bailaburg.

Mej. Watermaier read the document with care. She had obviously studied diligently the role of the professor's aged, virginal sister. Her grey hair was done up in braids which met over the top of her head; she wore a nondescript, brown dress that came well below her knees; her shoes were of the flat-heeled, lace-up variety. No stockings; shiny ankles. When she had finished the letter she folded it and put it back in the envelope, making no comment on its contents. "Will you come this way?" she asked. The door she led me through opened directly upon a room that ran the length of the severe, flat-fronted house. At one end of the room, on a dining-table, rested a plain open coffin. Irresistibly, she gestured me towards it.

The famous savant, mathematician, theoretician of science, teacher of morals, fighter for the rights of man, public scolder of the Phalanx and the Heerser, recipient of innumerable international prizes, and honoured expulsee from his last post at the Sixteenth of December University, lay on his back and presented to me a pinched, barely masculine version of his sister's face. His hands were crossed on his chest; he was dressed in a tweed suit appropriate either to countryman or academic. Staring down at him I wondered vaguely why death was always spoken of as lofty, grave, majestic, and so forth. It was nothing of the kind! Always in pursuit of new victims, always trying to achieve something worthwhile, it always ended up with the same paltry result.

Look at it!

So little, it seemed, prevented him from moving or speaking. Yet it was quite impossible to imagine him doing so. His skin must have been ruddy in life; now it was merely yellowish. There was a faint grey stubble on his cheeks. The features that would be the first to go showed up with a cruel clarity: the edges or rims of his lips and the open nostrils especially.

Mej. Watermaier had joined me at the side of the coffin. I did not know how long I was expected to stand there, and decided to let her make the first move. It was a mistake. She seemed ready to remain indefinitely where she was, gazing down at her departed brother. Eventually I stirred. I was just about to ask her, with as much reverence as the enquiry would permit, whether I should leave my car parked in the little drive at the front of the house, when she got in first.

"So now you're sorry for what you did to him?"

"I –"

"Now he can't harm you, you want to honour him?"

"I hope –"

"He would have sent you away. I know it. He wouldn't have had anything to do with you. But I have to make up my own mind now. He can't tell me what to do. I'm the only one who can say yes or no."

"Of course."

I was looking at her; she kept her flat, tear-bruised eyes on the body of her brother. Her hands, which held the letter, were working. Her old-maid shoulders rose and fell. "Why shouldn't everyone know what a great man he was? And what a loss – what a loss – what a – how much – we'll never –"

Convulsively she began to tear up the letter. With a demented gesture she threw the fragments at me. Some of them hit me, others fell to the floor, some fluttered into the coffin. I tried to restrain her, but she pushed my hand off her arm, and ran through to the rear of the house. I heard her going up some stairs. A door slammed, a bed or chair creaked. Then silence.

Needless to say, I felt a great fool. Also a little giddy, after the winding journey uphill to get to the place. I leaned over the coffin and began to pick up the pieces of paper that had fallen into it. The expression on the face beneath me seemed to have grown more severe, or perhaps just more depressed. The impulse to tweak the small, slightly aquiline nose of the great man we had lost suddenly rose up in me; too strongly to be resisted. It was much more rigid, more resistant, than I had expected it to be. With tingling fingers I picked up the rest of the paper from the floor.

The long room I stood in consisted of three distinct areas, each separated from the next only by a white-framed doorway leading to the rear. The coffin was in the dining section; next to it was a living-room with couch and armchairs; beyond a study, with bookshelves and a desk. Also a waste-paper basket, in which I threw the remains of the letter.

Then I inspected the books on the shelves. Stared out of windows. Sat in an armchair. Looked at a magazine. Inspected the professor again. Went back to the windows, one after another. Colours dulled as the sun climbed higher. The Enckelberg lost its purple hue and became blue, then grey, then hazy. A wind-pump over on one side briefly unfurled its steel vanes and kept them moving round together, like a juggler doing a trick; after a while it appeared to tire, and brought the performance to an end. For the tenth or twentieth time I looked at my watch. Hours to go.

By mid-morning, however, visitors had begun to arrive, and Mej. Watermaier had come downstairs again, outwardly as calm as she had been when she had greeted me. I thought there was an expression of sly satisfaction about her puckered mouth, with its thin moustache above. She had put me in my place. Now she could welcome her callers with a clear conscience. She had also, I noticed, donned a pair of thick stockings.

The locals mostly arrived on foot, in ones and twos; the Port Margriet contingent came by car, in a batch. All of them were sent to pay a visit to the coffin, first thing. The men sighed over it and set their lips; the women wiped the corners of their eyes with handkerchiefs. Flowers were deposited at the foot of the coffin; cakes were taken into the kitchen and then returned, cut into slices, along with the coffee-cups. In the democracy of mourning, villagers and professors' wives talked to one another in low voices. I was pointed out to everyone as "the special representative of the Prefect of Port Margriet" – whereupon people either avoided me or favoured me with ingratiating glances. My jaw had begun to ache from being set in an expression of reverent helpfulness. The charred, dark smell of coffee, which had seemed so appetising at first, had become almost sickening.

For all my impatience, however, the hearse actually came earlier than I had been told to expect it. They had done old Watermaier proud, I thought, when I saw the vehicle. It was a great old-fashioned affair, of a kind I recalled vaguely catching a glimpse of once during my childhood, on a visit to Vanir. The carriage at the back was all glass, incised with black fleur de lis and silver ribbons; around the top there ran a fretted, gothic rim of brass, cut into spikes and holes and little arches.

One of the sober-suited professionals who had arrived with it spoke briefly to Mej. Watermaier at the front door, then returned with his three assistants. Nodding from left to right, looking at no one, they rapidly threaded their way through the room, put the lid of the coffin in place (but did not screw it down) and lifted the burden upon their shoulders. The floorboards creaked under their weight as they carried it to the door. No other sound could be heard. The far end of the room, where the coffin had lain, looked naked all of a sudden: more desolate or pathetic, strangely enough, than when it had been there. The visitors exchanged glances, at a loss to know what to do next. Some of them hovered comfortingly round Mej. Watermaier, others made ready to slip away.

I went outside. The hearse had drawn up a little distance down the lane, because of the press of other vehicles parked directly in front of the house. The coffin had already been put into the back; it lay on view like something in a department-store showcase. The driver was just about to start the vehicle. I told him to wait for me. I was supposed to follow the hearse in my car.

"Wait?" He looked at the man on the seat beside him, and then at the two on the seat behind. "Our orders were to get back as soon as we could."

"Well, you've got to wait until I'm ready."

"Are you . . . family of the deceased?"

"No, I'm the Prefect's representative."

Again they exchanged glances.

"As you wish."

I went back to the house. Some guests were leaving. Mej. Watermaier was nowhere to be seen. I approached a rather large, bold-featured woman in clinging clothes of yellow and brown, who for some reason seemed more familiar to me than anyone else in the room, but whom I was to identify only much later. (Why I failed to recognise her seems a mystery to me now. Where were my eyes? My only excuse is that she was out of context; and so was I.) Anyway, it was her I chose to go to, among all the others.

"Is Mej. Watermaier upstairs?"

"Yes."

"Do you think she'll be long? The men are anxious to leave."

"I have no idea."

She turned away. So did I. Involuntarily my gaze went to the place where the coffin had rested. The view through the window at that end of the room was now unobstructed. At a distance of about fifty metres I saw the hearse slowly leave the side-track that led to the Watermaier house, and enter the scarcely wider lane to the village. My surprise at its departure became consternation when I saw that it was not turning left, towards the village and the main road to Port Margriet, but right, eastwards, towards the mountains.

Done! Lost! Swindled! I was out of the house in an instant, through a fence, across a field, running at an angle to the route the hearse was taking. It dipped and rose ahead of me like a great boat. Then it appeared to me like a crown, shining on the very brow of the country, with nothing but sky behind it. My feet laboured over stones, little thorn-bushes, goat-droppings, a kind of thin turf. In front of me was a low earth embankment, surmounted by a strand of barbed-wire. The barque with its precious cargo dipped again; but this time it came up much more rapidly than before. It was accelerating. They must have seen me. I reached the embankment. The hearse was speeding away down the track. Pale, dreamily vacant slopes gazed down at it from a distance; others, farther off, were not solid at all, merely hazy textures of light and colour.

I was fully aware of what a derisory figure I cut, even in the very moment I acted. Behold the bold bodyguard chasing the fugitive hearse through the empty landscape. See the body vanishing at an ever-increasing speed. See the student-undertakers grinning all over their faces at the success of their ruse. Now see the bold bodyguard, full of rage, take out his gun and fire desperately at the retreating vehicle. For the first time in his career he uses a gun. Why? To defend a corpse!

The noise of my first shot blotted out everything but itself. Some of the beautiful incised glass at the back of the hearse jumped up in a flurry. I fired again and again. My last shot appeared to be the lucky one. The vehicle slewed to the right, hit the embankment a glancing blow, and slithered along in furtive, animal-like fashion for a few yards, before coming to a stop. I thought it was done for, and began running once more. But it had halted for a moment only. Its engine raced. A lewd swirl of smoke emerged from its exhaust. Then it pulled away, putting on more and more speed. The hills instantly reappeared, as silent and motionless as before. All was quiet, except for the rapidly diminishing sound of the engine, and my own exorbitant panting.

I will not linger over what happened immediately afterwards. My dealings with the local police; my explanations to the hysterical Mej. Watermaier (her skin coarsened by shock, her eyes yellow with hysteria); the discovery early the next morning of the abandoned hearse at a crossroads about fifteen kilometres distant, with the corpse gone from it; my crestfallen return to

Port Margriet; the accusations and bitter sarcasms of the Prefect there; the recovery of the body from the basement of a students' hostel, to which the police were led by an informer; the interrogations I went through in Port Margriet and my despatch under escort to Bailaburg, in order to undergo further questioning there – all this, I thought, had finished me off for good. Bodyguard indeed!

XI

I was put into a room in the Old Remount School, in Bailaburg, and told not to leave it until further investigations into the affair were concluded. The sentries at the gate, I soon found out, had been instructed accordingly. On my first day there two men in civilian clothes, whom I had never seen before, came and took a statement from me. I repeated what I had already said many times to various interrogators in Port Margriet. Then I was left alone.

My room was quite comfortable. I was not quite under arrest, it seemed, even if I wasn't free to go. Equipped with a bed and a basin, the room overlooked a blond gravelled square, where the police horses had once been put through their paces. Now the place had fallen into disuse; it was all but deserted inside and out, day and night. Every time a door slammed the noise echoed voluminously down empty corridors and colonnades. I ate in a big, raftered hall, hung about with disintegrating banners, like webs, which hardly coloured the light that went through them. My table companions were a few taciturn guards, in militia uniform, most of whom appeared to be on the point of retirement, if not past it. Evidently they had orders not to talk to me. In the mornings and afternoons I was allowed to walk about in the square and to look through black iron railings at the tree-lined boulevard outside. Mist and sun conspired together to produce melancholy effects above the square: curdlings, concentrations, separations.

After a couple of days the same pair of investigators – the one beefy and expressionless, with eyes so small I could never see what colour they were; the other a moustached snuffler, a gnawer of his pencil – came and asked me questions again. The same questions. No, I had never met Professor Watermaier. No, I had never read any of his works. No, I had never communicated before with his sister. Yes, I was sure I would be able to identify the bogus undertakers who had called at the house; certainly the driver of the hearse, who had appeared to be their leader, and whom I had had a good look at.

The two men copied all this down yet again and departed. No-one else spoke to me. During those milky-blue mornings touched with gold, those grey and mauve evenings pierced by lamplight, those nights of silence interrupted at rare intervals by the sound of footsteps crunching on gravel, it occurred to me as a real possibility – for the first time, I might almost say – that perhaps I was not going to make a great success of my life. Quite apart from my anxiety about what was going to happen to me next, I was tormented by the image of that hearse forever retreating from me: the prone professor sailing to eternity upon it, and Josef Baisz, a sweating figure of farce, an unavailing idiot, pursuing it through the empty countryside. The absurdity of the picture, its low farcicality, was not its least depressing aspect.

I have already said that only that which a man dares to imagine ever becomes possible for him. If this is true of success, it is true also, I then realised, of failure.

The mist hung and moved within the square, it parted to reveal fluted pillars and pedimented hoods raised like eyebrows above rows of staring windows. The railings sweated clear drops, impregnated with metal even to the eye, let alone to the taste. (Yes, I did put my fingers to them and lick the moisture off.) The sky was closed overhead. Cars flapped over fallen leaves on the road with a curious, clumsy busyness. Another few days went by. Then I was summoned into an office on the first floor, where an unexpected visitor waited for me. It was my old friend Trager, from the Crescent Café. He glanced at me as if he had never seen me before. I felt almost the same about him, since it was the very first time I had seen him on his feet. They were surprisingly small for a man of his weight. He was wearing a round, black hat, also unfamiliar to me, like a stopper on a decanter. He had brought with him a paper which was stamped by one official, then counterstamped by another. A few minutes later I was being driven in a car, with Trager stuffed behind the wheel, to a destination which he would not reveal to me. I looked round at the bewilderingly busy streets as though I had been away from them for weeks, not days. Trager drove the car in an obstinately silent fashion. I could not get a word out of him.

However, our destination could not really come as a surprise to me, given the driver. The car halted outside the Compresecor building which I had entered only once before. In the foyer I was handed over by Trager to another man, who took me into Kerrick's office. It was as impersonal as before: ostentatiously smaller and shabbier, if I can put it that way, than the offices of innumerable people who did not have a tenth or a hundredth of his power. There was a different calendar on the wall from the last time I had been there; the same portrait of the Heerser.

I was left on my own for a few minutes. Then Kerrick entered, walking stiffly and briskly to his chair. Time, like a slow fire in whose invisible flame we all shrivel and char, had been doing its work on him, as on me.

It took him a while to come to the point. He had to deliver a lecture to me beforehand. Several lectures, in fact. The first was on one of his favourite topics: on how ordinary and unassuming a man he was, and how it was his "mediocrity" that had really made him suitable for the kind of work he did. "I fit in, you see, Baisz. I have a face that people don't remember. An unoriginal, methodical mind. A bit of training has done the rest – and luck, luck, luck. If you can call it luck to be involved in a stinking business like this." Had things gone differently he could have been a successful schoolmaster or land-surveyor. He was sure of it. But chance had decided otherwise. One event had led to another. "When you look back, you're always tempted to make a pattern out of what's happened to you. Isn't that right? Then you start to believe that the pattern preceded the events. That's precisely the danger. It makes you narrow and predictable. You try to arrange everything to agree with the pattern in your mind, and if it doesn't, you disregard it. At that point, you're finished. Certainly as far as we're concerned. Useless. You mark what I say, Baisz."

I tried my best to look like an obedient pupil. Then he began to talk about the power of the Compresecor. It had long arms. Big ears. Deep cellars, too. Had I ever been down in the basement of this building? No? Perhaps I should go, before I left. Just to have a look. He seldom went there, actually. He was too soft-hearted. He couldn't stomach it. It wasn't a place for ordinary folk like himself. Fortunately there were plenty of people who were eager for the kind of work that was done down there; and he had never been one to deny them their opportunities. Or their pleasures. Not when they were entitled to them.

Spasm. Laugh. A quick backward throw of both hands to his ears, a jolly little movement, as if in applause at the delicacy of his sensibility. Not to speak of the delicacy with which he had revealed it to me. Followed by some gloomy statements, apparently contradicting what had just gone before, about how cautious the Command had to be in using its power. People "outside" imagined that all it had to do was to give an order for this faction or that power-centre to be liquidated in the appropriate manner, and it could be done. But things had never been like that. If only they were! What a simple life he would lead! The truth was that strongpoints held by "opposition elements" had to be carefully sapped and mined. Individuals within such factions had to be weakened by all means available. It could take years to isolate a truly powerful group. Only then could it be destroyed. The leadership had to be protected throughout from accusations and misunderstandings. From premature revelations, too. Suitable tactics had to be worked out for each case. The right connections made. Especially in lenient times like the present. In the old days people in his position had more scope; they could act more freely. But not now. And in the old days you could be sure that those who were punished – stayed punished.

(Laugh.)

By this time he was on his feet, limping and rolling about the room as he talked, so that I had to turn in my chair to keep him in view. Finally, with chin tucked into neck below, and eyebrows raised above, he took up a strategic position in front of the portrait of the Heerser. From there he gazed portentously at me and made the announcement I had been brought to hear.

He had a job for me. A special job. A job within a job. If I did not take it up I would be returned at once to "a much less agreeable place than the Old Remount School" and would be left there to face whatever might be brought against me as a result of "the miserable balls-up – or worse" I had made over "old Watermaier". On the other hand, if I accepted his offer and did everything that would be asked of me, I'd hear no more about the Watermaiers, and I'd be well rewarded in addition. In cash. And in prospects of promotion.

"What is the job?"

"At the moment – as far as you're concerned – simply to work as driver and bodyguard for somebody we have our eyes on."

"Do I know him?"

"I doubt it."

"And what will I have to do – apart from driving and guarding?"

"You'll be told when the time comes."

"And now?"

"Nothing."

"I must take it on . . . sight unseen?"

"Exactly."

I had no more to ask.

He spoke again. "What's more, if you do take it on, and then let us down at any stage –!" He did not finish the sentence, but merely shook his head, staring at me from behind his spectacles, his blue eyes as alertly innocent as ever.

"What we have in mind eventually – later – won't be difficult for you to do. Unpleasant perhaps. But not difficult. You could call it child's play."

The silence between us was broken by the loudest and most explosive laugh I had yet heard from him. It was so convulsive I thought it would throw him over backwards. But he recovered and stood waiting for my answer, his eyes still twinkling with relish at the phrase he had used. I was to remember his mirth over it many weeks later.

By the time I got up to go I had accepted his offer. Of course. I felt some trepidation in having done so; but a great deal more relief. At last the call for which I had been waiting had arrived. The opportunity to prove myself before him meant even more to me at that moment than being done with the consequences of the Watermaier affair.

After I had thanked him and said goodbye he called me back unexpectedly, from the door. He had an enquiry to make. It was about the claims for expenses which Trager had been putting in. He had presented bills for fancy meals he was supposed to have had with various people – Josef Baisz included. Had I ever had such meals with him?

No? He shook his head regretfully. He'd thought not.

Still, Trager was a faithful soul. A fine worker. Not to be underestimated.

In silence we contemplated the virtues of Trager. Then, fingers playing an imaginary scale in the air, he dismissed me again. This time I was allowed to go.

I didn't ask the obvious question, after I had left the office with my new appointment in my pocket: why *me*? We never do ask that question about what we consider to be our good fortune. Only when circumstances turn against us do we suddenly recover our modesty and wonder why we have been singled out by fate. So it was in this case. Later it was to become obvious to me why I had been chosen; and why Kerrick had spoken so bitterly of how careful he had to be in "these lenient times". He had wanted somebody who was not directly in his employ to do this job for him. He had thought of me precisely because I was in a jam. Therefore I would oblige him. And I would be easier to disown than one of his own men, if things went badly.

Things did go badly for him: so badly that he never even had the opportunity to disown me. In the presence of hordes of others, I was to disown him.

XII

THUS, AS INSTRUCTED, I joined the household of Advocate-General Haifert and Mef. Haifert, bringing with me testimonials from several eminent people. One of these was the Prefect of Port Margriet, who presumably wrote about me just as he was instructed to, despite his long-standing friendship with the Advocate-General and his disgust with my past performance.

From my very first day, everything about the Haiferts and their beautiful apartment had in my eyes the pathos of inexpectancy, the fragile stillness that precedes a violent disruption. Those carefully chosen paintings by reputable modern artists on the white, well-lit walls; those bookshelves arranged so neatly by subject (his subject law, of course; hers literature); Katarina, the maid, who didn't like me; Barbara and Paarl, the children, who did – they were all equally under sentence. I had no idea what the sentence would be; no idea what "crime" it would punish; Kerrick hadn't vouchsafed information of this kind to me. But there was no doubt in my mind that I was there to put the sentence into effect. So I could afford to be patient and tolerant and generous with them. Even with Mef. Haifert, who treated me like dirt.

In view of subsequent events, I shall describe first how she, rather than her husband, struck me. Complete with long legs, small bosom, and strained mouth, she was one of those handsome, upright, serious-minded women who so often marry high-class academics. They reach their peak in their mid-thirties, I have noticed, just when their rivals begin either to bloat or to wither. She had met Haifert when he had been the youngest-ever Recktor of the Kamfersdam College of Jurisprudence; she had just graduated from the women's college of the university in Baila-burg. Now she lectured at the De Souter Institute of Fine and Practical Arts; she cooked; she managed the children firmly; she was always smartly dressed. In bed too, I suspected, her embraces were carefully thought out beforehand, provided at regular intervals, and brought to a prompt conclusion, with all the frank-ness and meanness of her kind.

As for Haifert himself – my initial impression was that he was more like a ham actor than a distinguished lawyer. That was my second impression, too. Everything about him was theatrical, self-conscious, convulsive: even his pallid cheeks, within which dark-ness came and went at moments of stress. His eyes and lashes were always a-quiver; he had the histrionic habit of running both hands backwards through his straight black hair, which always fell forward again; when he laughed, he half-closed his eyes and shook his shoulders, but produced no sound. His self-conscious-ness was so extreme that he sometimes put me in mind of a prisoner on the *qui vive* for his jailer's approach. He hears foot-steps, voices, clashing keys. He darts to the door. The jailer appears. It is himself.

But not this time. This time Josef Baisz is at the door: full of the bright, benign excitement of treachery, the lofty yet intimate pity of foreknowledge. Is there anything I can do for him? Did he call? Would he like me to –? With a strained attentiveness I listen to him; with alacrity I hasten to do his bidding; with self-effacing patience, indeed with humility, I return to make myself available once again.

There is nothing like it; no pleasure can compare with it. I speak as an expert. In such moments of exaltation, it even seems to you that you are doing your victims a favour. Through you they will come to know by what perversities and reciprocities the world is really governed.

Not only did my position in the household make me tolerant and gentle; even more paradoxically, perhaps, it made me incurious as well. It was a matter almost of indifference to me who Haifert's political friends were, who his enemies, and what role he and his office were to play in whatever schemes he was participating in. (His office had the primary function of vetting legislation put before the Chamber of Deputies; for historical reasons it was also the repository of the formal constitution of the Phalanx. Hence its "sensitivity".) All I needed to know would be revealed to me in due course. In the meantime I was content to go with him every day to the Palace of Justice, of which his bureau occupied one floor in the east wing; to return home with him at the end of the day; to play with his children; to listen to the provocations he continually offered me, and to provoke him in turn by never rising to them. It goes without saying that he and his wife distrusted me, notwithstanding all the recommendations with which I had come to them. That was exactly why he was always teasing me, trying to draw me out, daring himself to see how far he would go in my presence. He had to do it; it was his nature; he could help himself no more than I could. He was always lunging demonstratively at the truth, and thus sending it flying from him.

An example? One springs to my mind at once: so readily, indeed, that I pause, uncertain whether or not to put it down. The hindsight problem again. At the time I thought nothing of what he said. Later, when I was briefly at Ronaldsflai College, it seemed to have acquired an ironic significance. Now –?

Anyway, here goes. Haifert is at his desk; I am at the door. It is early evening. The curtains are drawn; the desk-lamp is on; his face in its light is very dark and very pale. His hair hangs down on both sides of his forehead. Wishing to relax after a spell of work, he does so by talking about himself, as is his wont. Do I know, he asks me, why he wanted to become a lawyer? No, I do not know why he wanted to become a lawyer. With a challenging but complacent smirk on his lips, and a higher-than-usual rate of oscillation of his eyes, he tells me.

"For the same reason that I wanted to go into the church when I was a little boy!"

Dutifully I express the surprise he obviously expects of me, on hearing that he had once cherished such an ambition.

"You see, Josef," he goes on to explain, "I wanted to be . . . good. Virtuous. Moral. Truthful. And I knew I wasn't. Far from it. So I figured out that if I became a pastor who stood up every Sabbath day and told everyone what to do, the problem would be solved. Then I would *have* to be good. Much later the idea of being a lawyer had the same kind of appeal. If I'm on the side of the law, then I must be a man of virtue, isn't that right?"

"I hope so."

"Even in a system like ours?"

"Especially in a system like ours."

He grins, watching himself rather than me, in some blinding, internal mirror. More lower lip; a glimpse of white teeth sloping inwards. "Ah, Josef, how very touching."

"Yes," I answer, declining to be provoked.

"I didn't understand, when I was a kid, that if you accept the lies you live by, then they become a kind of truth. Don't they? They must. The only truth you'll ever really know, anyway."

"That's too complicated for me."

"Is it, Josef? Is it really?"

All I can do to show how hard I am thinking is to blow out my cheeks, before nodding slowly. This display of stubborn stupidity bores him. With a slightly petulant air he picks up and holds out to me a few letters from the desk.

"Could you take these down to the box for me? I want them to get the last post."

On the way down in the humming, wood-panelled lift, which smelled curiously like a well-oiled gun, I looked at the names on the envelopes. None of them meant anything to me. The letter-box was just down the street from the entrance to the building. On the corner was the shop belonging to my friend, Nicky, whom I had come to know since moving into the apartment. Through the open door I could see him, in his apron, serving a housewife with a loaf of bread. The shop was so jammed with food of all kinds it didn't seem surprising that Nicky should be so fat. I ordered a cool drink from him, which I drank directly from the bottle, standing at the counter.

"So how's tricks?"

"Tricks are fine. And with you?"

"O.K. – no grumbles."

"That's the spirit."

"How about a game of cards this Saturday?"

"Sure. I can put the wife to work."

"For a change!" cried an indignant female voice from the room behind the shop.

Nicky grinned and winked at me.

"See you then."

I paid him with a coin that rang sharply on the old-fashioned counter: a slab of marble with blue veins running through it. During the few minutes I had been in the shop, the lamps in the park across the road had been switched on. They hung in long diagonal chains along the pathways, and met at a fountain in the middle. Flood-lit from below, suspended in mid-air, the fountain's white jets appeared motionless, like the snow-covered branches of a tree. At this distance it was impossible to distinguish the bronze nymph in the middle of the pool from the pair of dolphins with which she perpetually grappled.

Nicky was an enthusiastic, noisy player. That Saturday afternoon, as in all our games, never a card was put down without an accompanying groan or whoop; never a hand was dealt to him but he frowned over it and made little motor-bike noises between closed lips, busily shifting the cards back and forth. Through the open door to the shop I had a rear view of Nicky's wife reaching up to a shelf or stooping to bring out an item from under the counter. Children came from the park for ice-creams and chocolates. Servants from adjacent apartments, whose employers had gone away for the long weekend, bought polonies and loaves of bread and cartons of milk. Over and over again the cash register rang and its drawer slithered out like the tongue of a greedy animal, eager to swallow whatever was put on it. A great wad of the early edition of the evening paper was dumped down near the front door. Once Nicky had to abandon our game to help his wife deal with a drunk. He came back swearing perfunctorily and shrugging his shoulders. "Fuckin' people – pooh!"

Nothing more serious disturbed the calm, democratic opulence of that holiday afternoon. The next day was Founders' Day. No work on Monday. Who doesn't respond to the opportunities such weekends seem to offer? Life opens its hand. The hours drop through. Four o'clock. Five. Half past.

I put down a two of hearts, a seven of clubs, and a smiling knave with curled whiskers, a flat hat, and an axe in his hand. "That's the lot," I told Nicky. "I'm finished. I must go and get ready. Big night tonight. I'm dining with the Heerser, man. Don't expect me back."

Nicky proudly scooped up his winnings and threw the lot into the pocket of his denim apron. "That was good," he said. "It'll be better still next time."

I left promising to get my revenge, and Nicky followed me to the door, saying that it was only fair I should lose; he sat in his shop all bloody day and night, while I went to parties with all the big shots.

When I had walked down to the café soon after lunch the air had been clear; now it was yellow, cinnamon, mauve, with innumerable particles of dust seeming to float in it. On an impulse, I crossed the road and turned into the park. A severe oblong of a place, it was bounded on three sides by tall apartment blocks, and on the fourth by a railway cutting from which rumbles and groans could be heard intermittently. Everything was peaceful. Children ran. Parents walked. Dogs inspected other dogs. The dolphins vomited water into the basin of the fountain, drenching the bronze nude between them, who held up her face ecstatically to the setting sun. A crazy old man who was there every weekend paraded about with a placard on his back and pamphlets thrust into the band of his ancient hat. He had some feud going against the authorities; but the police left him alone; he wasn't worth bothering about. Behind him, at a distance of about twenty paces, was his constant shadow: a woman as old as he, and even thinner and shabbier, who never said a word but devoured him with lovesick eyes. A tram swayed and clanged down the street on the far side of the park, the imperiousness of its passage absurdly diminished by distance.

I had taken my usual place on a bench near the fountain. The noise of rushing water was like a canopy, sheltering me, permitting my thoughts to go wherever they liked. They went nowhere. A pair of lovers on the grass exchanged the occasional nuzzle and nibble. A park-keeper walked by, ringing a hand-bell: closing time in fifteen minutes. The noise staggered out of the mouth of the bell and failed spasmodically. Someone came and sat down next to me: someone heavy: the bench yielded perceptibly under his weight.

It was Trager.

"You'll be at the reception tonight?" he asked.

I nodded.

"Good."

He was carrying his round hat in his hand. He stared deeply into it. "I've been waiting for you all bloody afternoon." He put his hat on his head, his ears at once vanishing inside it, and waddled away, without another word.

XIII

THE PLACE: the Hall of the People. The occasion: a Founders'
Day reception. My position: a lowly one, near the door, looking in.

With its lofty profusions of scarlet and gilt, marble and cream,
the hall is like a great galleon, sailing endlessly through the sea of
time. No-one there has seen the distant decades that lie astern, or
will see those that lie ahead; we have all been taken aboard for one
brief journey only. But our voices rise loudly to the remote, full-
bellied ceiling, as if it is our breath alone that drives the vessel
forward. Presently, after a yell and a stamping of feet outside, and
a murmur and shuffle within, we fall completely silent. The
Heerser has just entered.

Why should it be so astonishing that he looks exactly like his
own picture? I don't know. It just is. Even after all the time I have
spent in Bailaburg I am still amazed to see that the head on all
those posters and coins has a single living original. His jaw juts
out heavily from narrow temples, as if it is soldered to his cranium
at the two knots of bone just below his ears. He wears a khaki
uniform with a single star on his breast. His hair is greying and
brushed up straight, in a military cut; the effect is to make him
appear ascetic, unsparing of himself. Everybody's eyes are fixed
on him; he looks at no one. Or rather, he seems to be looking for
a particular point among us, the secret centre of the crowd,
which only he can recognise.

Let him come closer. Across his barbered, dangerously compressed temples run a few veins. They are fine but charged with blood; pale blue; alive. His eyes stare beyond you. Their irises are like mica: tawny in colour, scratched within, laid plate by tiny plate around the pupil. A mineral eye.

His smile is sudden and overwhelming, revealing small, boyish teeth. The jaw beneath remains set; the eyes unchanging; the temples taut.

This one. That one. A salute acknowledged here. A curtsey there. A handshake. A bowed head. A smile. Now it is the turn of this junior officer. Now of that ageing official. They step back with suffused faces, breathing a little more heavily than before, full of embarrassed pride at having been chosen for greeting by their ruler. State Heerser. Director of the Phalanx. Chairman of the Centraad. Commander of the Armed Forces.

Finally he reaches the platform. He pushes aside the microphone which a flunkey proffers to him, and speaks directly to us, leaning forward with his hands on hips as he does so. Founders' Day, he tells us, is a day of rejoicing and re-dedication for country and Phalanx alike. It is a charge we make to our children, as a sign of the freedom that comes unsullied to their hands. On this day we read, revere, and uncover the names of the Founders who gave our freedom to us. To defend it is the sole task he has set himself; when it ceases to be so he will cease to be our Heerser.

Tighter and higher than when he speaks to a smaller group, his voice contains a vibration which seems to be plucked as much from our bodies as from his vocal chords. So we do not merely listen to him, but are compelled to participate in the physical effort of his speech. When he brings his words to an end with a characteristic abrupt, chopping gesture, there is a moment's silence before we dare to applaud. Then we clap our hands furiously together: performing, it would seem, a ritualistic winnowing of some kind, isolating him, freeing him from all husks and encumbrances.

Now he leaves the platform and passes once more between us, on his way to attend other celebrations that are taking place elsewhere tonight. His entourage follows. Esselen, his political secretary. Kroll, his aide-de-camp. Prahaan, his chef-de-protocol.

Heefer, his equerry. Tromp f'n Eyskens, his pathic. And several bodyguards, some of whom are acquaintances of mine. They pass out of the doors; behind them, within the hall, a murmur of conversation, soft at first, then rising in volume, begins again.

Soon it has become as loud as before. Wondering when my summons will come, and what form it will take, I try to watch the entire assembly, the entire crew. Judge Illuxt, my boss's boss, an over-grown, bespectacled hulk of a man, with something infantile about his appearance, especially about the way he throws his feet jerkily forward and only then seems to follow them, makes a clumsy pathway through the throng, straight towards me. Is he the one? But no, it seems that he is only going to the lavatory. On my right an old gentleman, with the ribbon of the Ox-Wagon Order in his lapel, peers attentively down the dress of a girl less than half his age, and says with a hopeless attempt at roguishness, "You have the most wonderful attributes!" He lisps slightly over the last, carefully chosen word. The girl raises a brow, despising him for the remark, yet willing to hear more. Elsewhere I see white shirt-fronts, the glint of glasses, the bare arms of women, uniforms, faces. On the far side of the hall stewards in buff-coloured linen tunics have begun to bring forward long tables which they proceed to cover with cloths and cutlery. Kerrick, whom I have not spotted among the rest, touches me on the shoulder and whispers a word or two in my ear. A few minutes later I follow his instructions, and go into a little room to the side of the hall. He is already there, waiting for me; and so is someone else. An old acquaintance.

A very old acquaintance. It was my cousin, Anton.

He had changed greatly since I had last seen him. Even his name had changed. He was now called "Pieter". At any rate that was how Kerrick, who obviously did not know of the connection between us, introduced him. Nor did Anton recognise me. But I knew him at once, though he had grown into a big, swarthy man, with a flat, shield-shaped face and a pair of violently black brows running in a bar across it. His hair was carefully combed back, so carefully that the track left by each tooth of the comb was still clearly visible; his skin was the dark red colour of the polished granolithic stoops of my childhood; his eyes still had a light, demented flicker to them. He did not speak until he had heard what was wanted of us; then he smashed his clenched fist loudly into the palm of the other hand and yelled out, "We gonna give 'em the zu-zu-zap!"

Kerrick was scandalised by the noise. I was startled too. I did not know then how often I was to hear from him that yell, that threat or war-cry. He cheered himself up with it, he menaced others with it, he used it to describe a fight, a fuck, a big meal, his glowing future, almost anything.

The prospect that had so excited Anton was indeed child's play, as Kerrick had promised it would be, when he had first offered me the job. Literally so. We were to seize the Haifert children and hold them in captivity in a place the Compresecor had hired for the purpose. My position in the family would make their abduction easy enough to carry out. It was essential that it be done peacefully, quietly, with no alarm raised.

The purpose of the operation was none of our business; but Kerrick was prepared to say a certain amount about it. Haifert, he told us, was in touch with a "faction" led by certain personalities of even higher rank than himself, who were known to be plotting against the security of the state and the life of the Heerser. The time had come to "flush them out". How? By feeding them with incorrect information about the readiness of some members of the Heerser's entourage to cooperate with them. Haifert had been chosen as the channel for this information. He would know it to be false; nevertheless he would tell his friends exactly what he was instructed to say. Why? Because the Compresecor would be holding his children hostage. When the operation was successfully concluded, they would be released.

Anton grinned eagerly. By the working of his jaw and the clenching of his fist I could see he would have liked to express his approval more vociferously. But he did not dare to do it. I asked what would happen if Haifert refused to cooperate. Kerrick smiled. Haifert was a loving father. The question didn't arise.

And how long would the children be kept?

As long as proved necessary.

And Haifert?

No answer.

Bald, bespectacled, earnest, smaller than the two men to whom he was giving his orders and explanations, Kerrick looked like a family solicitor dressed up in his dinner-jacket for a big night out. His last words, however, were unmistakably those of a boss of the Compresecor. He would show us no mercy if we let him down in any particular. We were going to be held responsible for one another. Both would be punished for the mistakes of either. Was that clear?

Anton and I exchanged a glance. Yes, it was clear.

All this took place in a little room, like a verger's, to the side of the hall. It contained some wooden chairs pushed to one side, and a small table covered with a stained white cloth, with some empty bottles beneath it. Against a wall stood a brown cupboard, in which I remember suspecting that someone might be hiding. We left the room one by one. While we had been there, music had started up in the hall; I'd heard the strains in the intervals of Kerrick's speech, almost as if he had been conducting more than just our conversation with his energetic forefinger. Back in the hall I found the guests eating to the strains of a folk-orchestra.

Haifert and I left soon after. He chose to drive, as he often did when we were alone. Passing lights gave his face a fugitive solidity. Shadows raced round it like spokes. Our headlights scooped up the darkness, and let it overflow on both sides. At home Haifert used to talk to me compulsively. In the car he was silent. I fell into a kind of doze. Points of light swung behind my closed eyelids, and the road seemed to tilt itself into the air. I felt the coming and going of a soothing pressure as he took each corner.

Curiously enough, Haifert took me into his study when we got home, and for the very first time, almost as if he knew what had taken place during the reception, lectured me on the plans he and his friends had for "reform" and "re-moralisation" and "restabilisation" of the state and party. Magic words! He evidently believed in them; more, I think, than he believed in himself. All those chest-heavings, droopings of the head, teeth-grindings, fist-clenchings, grins at the carpet, and so forth, which he was compelled both to perform and to watch, even while talking privately to me – they not only exhausted him; they discredited him in his own eyes. But not his words. His words gave him faith.

More words. Stirring words. A renewal of realism. A productive economic order. Flexibility in party procedures . . .

He lunged upwards for breath with his whole body, like a drowning man. The air rattled as it went into his breast; then it was exhaled in a rush. Another lunge; another breath. The longer he went on the deeper became the pity I felt for him.

"You must be careful," I said, interrupting him in mid-sentence.

He was now seated at his desk; I was in an armchair to the side of it. He looked up and answered me mildly; calmed rather than startled by my warning.

"Oh, we don't intend doing anything unconstitutional."

"All the same – be careful."

He said, "I'm glad you're concerned."

I reached out and touched his sleeve. His red-rimmed eyes gazed down on my hand.

Time for bed. I left him there. I do believe that the hour we had spent together was to have its effect on us both, later. A very different effect, in each case. Even my sleep, when it came that night, was penetrated with tenderness for him, with a yearning emptiness, a light, tight sense of apprehension and excitement.

I know the question that will be asked at this point. I heard it then. I hear it now. How could I have done it? How could I have acted as I did, if I pitied him?

I had an answer, too, that once seemed to me quite conclusive. All I can do now is repeat it, for whatever it's worth.

Don't you see, if I had never betrayed him, I would never have had the chance of pitying him!

116

XIV

OUT OF THE random scraps of information that came their way; out of the arrangements and furnishings of their home; out of the moods and affections of their parents and the idiotic preoccupations of Katarina; out of the lights and shadows sliding across the ceiling of the nursery after they had gone to bed; out of school, street, and park, the children had put together a world full of anxieties and terrors, perhaps, and yet self-evidently what it had to be, complete, wholly rounded upon itself. Solemn Paarl, with his precocious spectacles on his nose; slender Barbara, her mother's daughter even to the quiver of her nostrils; both of them with such bare, frail necks . . . What I had always found most touching about them was not their innocence, so to speak, but their knowingness.

There was no problem about picking them up after school. They climbed into the car eagerly. Barbara had a little purse slung by a cord over her shoulder; Paarl had tied his jersey-sleeves around his waist, so that the body of his jersey fell over his bottom, like a kind of apron in reverse. All the little boys in his school went about like that; it was a craze. Their faces were flushed and silvery from exertion. They sat in the seat next to me, while I drove in the opposite direction from the one I would have taken if I had been going home. They did not notice. They were too busy talking. There were two bad things that had happened at school, Barbara announced in her precise housekeeper's or accountant's manner, and proceeded to tell me what they were. Paarl was talking about a game he had played with Hans and had won.

Only when I stopped the car at a corner and Anton climbed into the back, as arranged, did they fall silent. They stared at him, overawed by his size and by the fierceness of his face. He began to give me directions. Take the Herleer Road. Turn right past the factory. Keep on the N13.

We must have travelled for six or seven minutes before Paarl asked me, in a small voice, "Why aren't we going home?"

"Because you're going to visit someone who wants to meet you," Anton answered.

I felt the convulsion of his frame in the seat behind me, even before I heard the sound of his fist meeting his palm. Then came the yell.

"He's going to give you the zu–zu–zap!"

Glancing sideways I saw two small, rigid faces turned to the back of the car, where Anton was still heaving about.

"We're going to have a little holiday in the country," I said. "Your mummy and daddy had to go away for a few days, and they've asked me to look after you."

They believed me and they did not believe me. They understood what was being done to them and they did not understand it. They were filled with fear and they laughed.

I drove on.

What I never expected from the children, then or later, was silence. Obedience. Submissiveness. Love.

True, we gave them sleeping pills every night, and these helped to keep them drowsy throughout the day too. But even before they took the pills with the milk, on the very first evening, they were quiet. When we arrived at the farmhouse Barbara went under a table in the front room. It was only when she caught her breath, with a long, shuddering sob each time, that you could hear she was crying. Paarl walked through to one of the rooms behind, trying to look unconcerned, a grin like a plaster stuck on his face. I found him sitting on one of the iron bedsteads in the room, staring fixedly at the torn cover of a magazine, which he must have found lying on the floor. Anton, who had followed me, screwed up the weather-beaten skin around his eye to give me a wink. "Heh! Kids!"

Presently I took them out of the house for their first walk. Barbara put her hand in mine, unbidden. The sun was setting. A single bird cried over black and purple fields. A faint breeze nudged at us. Down on the road a car ran helter-skelter towards the huge, motionless furnace of clouds in the west. Wind. Emptiness. The bird's cry. Barbara shivered and said, "It's very big in the country."

Inside there was a box of groceries on the table in the front room: tinned meat, tinned milk, bread, coffee, sugar. There were blankets on the beds. There were even packs of cards, and board-games for the children. (Ludo and snakes-and-ladders.) Anton told me proudly that he had been in charge of all these purchases. We used the lot during the days and nights that followed. It is now impossible for me to sort out those days and nights, one from another; it was difficult enough then. Broken nights. Long mornings. Longer afternoons. I remember the children sucking at holes punched into tins of condensed milk. Anton smoking. Barbara, thumb in mouth, lying on her bed and rocking to and fro, producing an identical noise from the springs each time: *earth-speak*, *earth-speak*, *earth-speak*. The sun hanging motionless in the centre of the sky, as if it had arrived at its destination and now had nowhere else to go. The moon extracting and mixing metals out of the clouds around it: silver, copper, bronze, pewter. Now Anton groans from his bed, "Oh! Oh! Oh!" before shooting out his legs and turning over to one side. In that position his groans are smaller and higher, more like whimpers. (Once when he was lying naked on top of the bed, I saw his hands steal down to his cock; the moment he touched it, his groans started up again, at full volume.) From the next bedroom Barbara begins to cry. I get up and give her a drink of water. A shake of the shoulder for Anton, to shut him up. "What? What?" He gulps and snorts a few times, rearing up in the half-darkness, before lying down again. The sky, tinged with the faintest green light, separates itself from earth; the stars vanish; sunrise exposes millet-fields, steel wind-pumps, the main road with its telegraph-poles about a kilometre down the slope. Farther off, at great distances from one another, are a few small, whitewashed farmsteads like the one we are in, each with a clump of dark trees standing sentinel around it. Another day.

Thus we gave them the zu-zu-zap.

To wound and to love; to love what I wounded; to betray and look pityingly upon the consequences of my treachery; and to do it again – and again – and again – and each time as if for the very first time, with a trembling, magnetised sense of fate or inevitability upon me: that was my addiction. And like any other addict I dreamed that precisely that which enslaved me would enable me to burst through the walls of circumstance, through the confines of the self, into a realm of unconditioned freedom.

But look at the complication of such enslavements! Because I loved the children I tried to avoid them, so far as it was possible in that house. But Anton, my accomplice, the tormentor of my childhood and now the tormentor alongside me of these children, I simply loathed. Moreover, I cherished that loathing zealously, like a plant or pet.

It grew rapidly. Almost everything he did nurtured it. Soon it seemed always to have been there, from our very first evening together. In the course of that first evening, incidentally, I had told him who I was. The revelation had fallen rather flat. Since I had last seen him his life had been so haphazard he was quite incapable of much surprise at any turn it took. During the days and nights that followed I heard more than I wished about his adventures. One version of them was all lies. Abject, childish lies. He had been an officer in the army. A medical student. A journalist "on one of the big papers". The other, truer version of his career emerged inadvertently or accidentally, as it were. There was a bloke on this building site – he'd been doing gardening for that rich *ouck* – the doctor in the hospital – no, not that hospital, the other one, where they sent him for psychie-something – so he buggered off –

I was in no position to look down on him. That did nothing to abate my hatred of him. On the contrary. Nor was I mollified by the fact that his recollections of our relationship in Vliss were so different from my own. We were good pals then, weren't we? Now we were pals again. Hey, wasn't that right? One day we'd be in the big-time. Then we'd give them the zu-zu-zap.

Bang. Fist in palm. Grin above. Red Indian forehead creased. Eyes vacant.

Soon I was almost as obsessed as he was with that bit of gibberish, and its accompanying gesture. So I provoked him to use it; I taught it to the children; I yelled it out into the empty countryside; I woke up at night from obscure dreams and found it on my lips. It was only a matter of time before I felt as if I had been called into the world to give *him* the zu-zu-zap.

He did not positively maltreat the children, apart from the occasional slap; that I must say for him. Nor did he resent the favouritism they showed to me: appealing to me for protection when he spoke to them, turning towards me their dazed yet naked eyes, making ingratiating movements in my direction with their knees and shoulders. If anything their appeals pleased him, for they showed that he was more the man of the two of us; he even took to calling me "mother", I remember. Which was another reason for me to hate him.

Whether I would have felt differently if we had had any word from Kerrick (even if it had just been to tell us to hold on), I do not know. But there was nothing. No messenger. No hint on our little radio of any special developments. No newspapers. The world had shrunk to the four of us, locked forever in that curtainless, carpetless little house, thrust down on the bare countryside. One of us a random, restless psychopath. Another, Josef Baisz, the well-known specialist in love and betrayal. And two terrified children: one with blue eyes, one with brown. Looking back, it surprises me it took so long for me and Anton to come to blows.

Morning. Afternoon. Evening. Night.

On the sixth morning (I think it was the sixth morning, but can't be sure) it began to rain, straight down from high, even clouds, with a silver light behind them. The rain was invisible against the sky, since the light was so strong; you could see the streaks of it only when they showed against the earth. Thicker dribbles fell here and there from leaking gutters. There was no other noise. Anton stood at a window, staring out at the rain and smoking a cigarette. With every puff he extended his cheeks, before ingesting the smoke; then he made a funnel of his lips and blew out against the glass. Barbara started rocking on her bed in the next room. Paarl lay on his back under the table, where I was sitting: a favourite place of his. *Earth-speak, earth-speak, earth-speak*. I was carefully shading in with a pencil all the wholly enclosed letters or parts of letters in the headline of an old newspaper. B – A – O – P – D – R –

The rain came down. The gutters ran incontinently. Anton ground out his cigarette on the window-sill. Paarl wriggled out from under the table and stood next to me, to see what I was doing. The hair at his temple tapered to a wisp under the thin metal bar of his spectacles. I put my arm around his shoulders and drew him closer to me. His body yielded to my embrace, his leg touched mine. I could feel the small warmth of it through my trouser-leg. Still staring out of the window, Anton said, "Hey, sonny, come and look at this."

I don't know what had caught his attention. I was never to find out. Nor was Paarl. Out of perversity, simply, I tightened my grip on the boy's shoulders.

Anton turned to look at us. He frowned, not very fiercely.

"Hey, come here!" he said again to Paarl.

I held him as tightly as before. Seconds passed; or seemed to pass. I could feel the child begin to tremble a little under my arm.

"I can't," he said.

Anton beckoned him forward. He struggled feebly, unconvincingly, against my grip. His eyes suddenly glistened behind the lenses of his glasses. Watching, Anton suddenly became enraged.

"You let the kid go!" he shouted. It took two strides, and his triangular, mask-like face was over the table, closer to mine than it had ever been before.

"Zu-zu-zap?" I asked politely.

That was all that was said by either of us, before he picked up the table from underneath, by its frame, and tried to overturn it on me. The crash as it hit the floor was followed by an astonishing, protracted silence. I had jumped clear. Paarl had slipped away and run into the next room. Anton stood within the ineffective cage of the table's protruding legs.

"You're a madman," I said over the barrier between us. "You were fucking crazy when you were at school, and you're even crazier now."

He backed away, keeping his eyes on me, and came round the side of the table. His hand went to his hip pocket. From there, with the action of a man throwing a quoit, he swept his arm towards me. Too late, I saw the little gleam at the end of his fingers. Something hard, something bad, happened to my shoulder. I kicked out at the same moment, and found him – I don't know where. He doubled over and I kicked out again. This time the point of my shoe reached his face. The noise it made was quite distinct from the sharp crack within. He screamed, and blood started out of his mouth, and trickled between his fingers. Hands to mouth, he declined slowly, and I pushed or shoved at him with my knee before sitting down next to him on the floor. Overcome with dizziness and fear I watched the blood running down my arm. The edges of my vision darkened inwards. Darkness filled my mind. When I opened my eyes I saw the children, at a great distance, in the door of the room. Both of them were crying. I hardly knew who they were. Anton, still kneeling on the floor, was rocking back and forth, making a noise. The table lay stupidly on its side, its legs thrust outwards, like a dead beast's.

Holding on to my shoulder, I struggled to my feet, went into the next room, and picked up a cloth which I put against my wound. Then I found one of my vests and looped it round and round the wad I had made. If I kept my arm close to my side, it would hold. I had no idea what to do next; except, vaguely, to go and see what Anton was doing; perhaps to help him if he was really badly hurt. It seemed a great labour to think even that far ahead.

Then the children sent my thoughts flying in quite another direction.

"Now we can go!" Paarl cried, grabbing at my wrist.

I looked from him to his sister: two small, stricken faces lifted in wild hope and fear to mine.

Of course! A sob or laugh rose in my breast like an eructation, squeezing everything but one new idea out of my consciousness.

With a jerk of my arm I threw Paarl off and ran through the front door of the house. The space and light outside came upon me explosively; but silently too. The rain had stopped. Only a few drops still trickled or ticked down from the roof.

The children had shot out after me. "Josef!" they were screaming. "Don't go away! Take us with you! You're our friend." Anton stood at the window, his hand to his face.

I turned on the children and charged at them with my arm raised. They scattered. By the time I reached the door of the car they were back at me again. Cursing and shouting, I managed to get inside and to shut them out. The engine started at once. With a blare of the horn, and a long splash and squelch from the tyres, I began reversing down the unmade track that led to the main road. The children ran with the car as far as they could, screaming and waving their hands. But they were soon left behind.

XV

IT WAS NOT UNTIL I got to Dronfeld Woods, on the outskirts of the city, that I came upon my first road-block. There it was, all of a sudden, round a curve in the road.

I didn't seem to take the decision about what to do; rather, the decision took me. (It may well have saved my life, in view of the political changes which had begun to take place while I had been incommunicado in the farmhouse.) Knowing nothing, acting on impulse, I stopped the car and simply dived into the trees to the side of the road.

There were yells behind me and the sound of running feet; followed by a couple of shots that passed wide and high, but very busily, over my head. I kept on running. Trees came at me like vengeful people, hissing and throwing up their arms. Twigs whined in my ears and slashed salt blows at my eyes. The earth humped itself up to trip me; then it went soft; then it disappeared entirely, only to swing from below, through concealing leaves, at my knees and outstretched, plunging hands. When I paused, hanging on to a branch, trying to listen for my pursuers, my heart-beats felt as if they were going to shake me to pieces. My chest produced notes I had never heard before. The men shouted and I turned to run. At the end of an ascending tunnel of branches I saw what looked like a steep, open, greenish slope. It grew and grew as I ran towards it; then it flexed itself hugely and opened out to become the sky.

I spent the night in the woods. It was horribly cold. My shoulder throbbed, burned, wept blood. The next morning I telephoned Gita from a booth on the side of the road. She responded to my appeal.

Several days later, when the radio announced that all banks and public offices were reopening for a few hours, I went to a safe-deposit vault in the middle of town, in which I had hired a tray a couple of years before. In that tray I had accumulated, bit by bit, a small, secret stock of articles. Its nucleus was the pistol Serle had given me when I had first come to Bailaburg, which no one had thought of asking me to surrender after I had left his service. Subsequently I had added some of the more expensive gifts that had come my way (as a reward for putting Landdrost Ericksen to bed, night after night, after he had drunk himself insensible; or for helping the State Actuaris, of all people, to locate a supply of under-age girls); some samples of stationery from a variety of government offices; blank identity cards I had stolen from the Ministry of the Interior; party membership cards; government rail warrants; incriminating love-letters to the wife of one of the people I had guarded (which I had never used); and various other articles.

Invaluable box! Invaluable property! I left the gun and much else where they were. I took only what I needed. In the reading-room of a public library nearby I gave myself a new identity by carefully filling in and signing a card. Then I took a bed in a flea-bag hotel not far from the main railway station.

There I remained for many weeks. Months, indeed. There were three other beds in the room, so I shared it with a succession of transients of the inevitable sort: small, fierce men on their way to or from worthless jobs, who guarded their cardboard suitcases with paranoiac fervour and furtiveness; several drunks and palsied old men; one outright lunatic with a tea-towel carefully pinned over his hair and a sneer of contempt for all around him fixed forever on his twisted lower lip; boys running away from home. Others among my room-mates were no more than a light switched on in the small hours, a cough, a smell of socks, a rumpled bed already vacated when I opened my eyes in the morning.

There was no reason for me to rise early. My time was my own. I got to know the city's parks and libraries better than I wanted to. Some afternoons I just used to remain in the room, when no-one else was there, lying on my bed. The setting sun shone through the smudged window; its warmth evoked smells of sour bodies and frayed blankets. From downstairs, where there was a bar and billiard-saloon much frequented by soldiers on leave, there came a yelling of songs and arguments, interrupted by intervals of uncanny silence.

Since I am writing an autobiography and not a history, the political changes which took place during those months are not really my subject. Everyone who follows the politics of our fatherland knows that the suicide (or murder, as some said) of Advocate-General Haifert precipitated a struggle for power which had little directly to do with his death, but with whose consequences we are in some sense still living. That the Heerser would be compelled briefly to give up his position, before resuming it with even greater powers than before; that the Compresecor would be declared a counter-revolutionary organisation, working with agents of a foreign power to undermine and overthrow the Phalanx; that the bodies of several members of the Directorate and Centraad, Judge Illuxt and Cornet-General Cillie among them, would be found floating in the Baila River; that yet another millenarian sect promising the Kuni people immunity to bullets and bombs would spring up among them and lead to renewed blood-letting in the mountains – how flattered and amazed my former employer would have been to have his name associated with such events!

Yet having known him as well as I did, I am sure he would have chosen a longer life before such glory, if only he had felt the choice to be open to him.

For myself, I lay low. The upheavals the country was going

127

through made it easier for me to do so. The only public event I took an active part in, along with thousands of other citizens of Bailaburg, was the sacking of the Compresecor headquarters, one hot autumn morning. As troops hurried the captured members of the Compresecor out of the building and into waiting trucks, you may be sure that I howled and spat and shook my fists quite as energetically as everyone else in the flailing, thrusting mob around me. The sky glittered with yellow motes; burned-out carcasses of vehicles grovelled in the street. "Assassins!" we yelled. "Dogs! Scum! Filth!" Emerging into the roaring sunlight, trapped in the space between the heaving walls of the crowd, the prisoners looked dazed and terrified, yet also pathetically in earnest about what they were doing, grotesquely eager to oblige, as if anxious to avoid committing a solecism in the wholly novel situation in which they found themselves.

Kerrick was among the first to come out. Such a jerky little man he suddenly appeared to be; so particular about where he was putting his feet. Perhaps he was concerned about his dignity; perhaps he was afraid that if he fell he would never be allowed to get up. I was in the front row of the mob; and he saw me there. I'm sure of it. Our eyes met. I yelled louder than ever and stretched out my hands, my hooked fingers, as if to strangle him. He looked away. Later Trager was hauled along like a fish. Bastard! Spy! Traitor! To the gallows with him!

Once the prisoners had been driven away, after much hooting, banging, swinging about with rifle butts, and even the firing of a few shots in the air by the troops, only a meagre guard was left behind to protect the building. I was in the first group to burst through the cordon; among the first to overturn a filing-cabinet inside and put a match to the papers that spilled out of it. The guards ran about yelling that they had been ordered to protect the documents we were destroying. But my example was followed by many others. Soon we had a most satisfactory blaze going. "Death to the documents!" we cried. "Long live the Armed Forces Purification Grouping!"

I returned to my room when I'd had enough of the excitement.

I heard later that a student had died in the fire; but that may have been just another of the unfounded rumours that were constantly going around the city at the time. Knowing that so many of the Compresecor's records had been reduced to ashes made me feel much safer, I must say, than I had before.

One of the most curious aspects of times of political crisis in my experience, however, is their calm, not their disorder; their tedium, not their violence. For the most part people simply seem to feel themselves suspended, at a loose end. They go to work, or they do not, as circumstances permit; their jobs, like all their other commitments, have become provisional, subject to instant abandonment. But the energy thus withdrawn cannot be promptly put to use elsewhere; it remains undischarged and attentive. The very air seems emptier than usual, except when it carries the sound of gunfire or loudspeakers; streets have the look of theatrical façades; people drift and loiter, when they can do so, keeping each other under observation with an almost village-like candour. They no longer know what their roles will be when they see each other next, or to what purpose these buildings and street-corners will be put. They are waiting to find out.

I saw no-one I knew during this time. No, that's not strictly accurate. Sitting in Jobber Park one day, fairly soon after I had got back to Bailaburg, I noticed a couple of vans being loaded with furniture outside the Haiferts' apartment block. Mef. Haifert and the children were watching over the job. So! They were safe. It was the first I had learned of their fate since I had abandoned them in the farmhouse. Needless to say, I did not try to find out more at that stage.

The Serles too I avoided, as I avoided all my other acquaintances. Here, however, I should explain why the tormented separation between Gita and myself, which had taken place in that wintry park, had not been irrevocable, as I had fully expected it to be. The explanation is quite simple. Gita had discovered since then that she adored me with an even deeper and more tragic love than before. Why? Precisely because I had thrown her saintly husband downstairs!

I put it coarsely. But it is the truth. She had convinced herself that her responsibility for the crime was equal to mine; she admired me for the depth of the passion I had revealed in committing it; she admired herself for rousing such passion in me; she believed us to be bound together forever by the guilty secret we shared. Bound together on the highest plane, needless to say. With plenty of sad smiles, quivering lips, distant gazes, and pure, pacifying touches of the hand. And only the occasional lapse, when circumstances favoured it, and we rolled together on the matrimonial bed, ramming our hairy loins together like any other ordinary, unregenerate couple.

Yet she was bound equally to Serle. The more our guilt united the two of us, the more it united the two of them as well. (I have already remarked on how romantic she was.) She had to protect him and nurse him and keep him in ignorance of what had been done to him. Not least of the reasons why she owed him all this was the striking spiritual transformation he had undergone, as a result of the misfortune that had befallen him.

He had got religion, if you please. He was now humble and penitent. Compliant to the will of God. Ashamed of the worldly ambitions he had pursued for so long. Anxious to convert me to his way of thinking. Striving to be content with his new lowly position in the personnel department of the state electricity corporation. I couldn't help feeling that he remained as simple-minded in his new faith as he had ever been; he was still sustained by the conviction that sooner or later he would again be rewarded simply for being there, on the spot, available to the authorities. But the authorities he now turned to were a different set from the last.

The relationship between the three of us, anyway, had thus settled down into a pattern of long absences and brief, charged meetings. Once, I remember, on a visit to the little flat they now lived in – in the fern-embowered house of a creepily cordial tax-inspector – I was provoked by Serle's constant preaching at me into telling them of the only intimation I had ever had of the existence of God. It had come when I'd been working for Mr

Kitzinger, back in Vliss. In the Universal Library of Famous Literature I had come across a passage in which some French philosopher had argued for the reality and veracity of the external world on the grounds that God would not use the senses he had given us in order systematically to deceive us. Lucky Frog! Putting the book down I stared through the open office-door, across the deserted village square. The God whose presence seemed to suggest itself to me there, in the afternoon's suddenly attentive stillness, its glittering silence and vacancy, was of a very different kind. His nature was revealed in the unremitting practice of deception and betrayal. Behind spectacle, suffering, variety, the overwhelming conviction each of us had of the importance of our own experiences, was nothing. Emptiness. Negation. Death. Fraudulence.

All one could do was to try and get in first.

Serle, the man I had cuckolded and crippled, solemnly shook his large head and put his hands to his ears, so that he would not hear more of what I was saying. The man who could be called a living instance of the truth of my words, and who thanked his God for having made him realise "what was truly important in this life", told me that he pitied me. Behind him, his wide-eyed spouse shook her head sadly. Her gaze was as expressive and full of light as ever. Only, just beneath the iris of her left eye a small red fleck had appeared. It looked as if some tiny missile from outside had starred the sclera, like a pane of glass; or as if the heat and pressure within had made its first breach there.

This discussion had taken place long before I'd gone to work for Haifert; long before I'd kidnapped the children and abandoned them to Anton. I mention it here because during the protracted spell of inactivity just described I realised two important facts about myself. They were so simple I was amazed I had managed to avoid them before. They were so appalling in their implications, however, I knew exactly why I had for so long refused to recognise them.

First. In some deeply hidden, childishly expectant part of myself, in some hitherto unreachable (and unteachable) chamber of my soul, I had been cherishing a hope that if I served my God of falsity and double-dealing with sufficient zeal, if I did all he could possibly ask of me, he would in the end, reward me. Not just with excitement and worldly advantage and a sense of accomplishment; but ultimately, and above all, by discharging me from his service. By setting me free. By letting me serve a less demanding master.

Second. He was never going to do it.

XVI

I HADN'T BEEN IN TOUCH with my sister for a long time; nor had I heard anything from my mother. When conditions finally settled down, with the new or revised administration firmly in control, and no indication from any source that I was a wanted man, I resumed my original identity and headed north, back to Boschoff. Besides, my money was exhausted.

I found Beata and Fenter living in the same flat as before. They had a new baby: another girl, like the two older children. I found, too, that at Beata's instigation my mother had sold the shop in Vliss and moved not far from the Fenters. She had a little room in a house full of cats and other old, peering women, who lived like her on their meagre state pensions. She was shrunken and subdued. One eyelid drooped; one finger trailed along walls when she walked down a street or corridor.

"You're back," she said to me by way of greeting. "I wondered when you'd be back."

Then she lost interest in my return. Later she complained to me about feeling useless, having nothing to do, waiting to die. "I never thought I'd live so long!" she exclaimed; and as she said it her eyes filled with tears and she puffed out her wrinkled cheeks, like a child trying to stop herself crying.

She meant it; yet she didn't really say it to me; I just happened to be her audience at that moment. For the rest, her big pre-occupation was making sure of the supply of pills she received from the dispensary of a local hospital. Christ knows what was in them, or how many of them she used to take at a time; but they enabled her to sit motionless for long periods, whether in her room or in Beata's flat.

Beata, by contrast, made a great fuss of me. She always did, whenever I turned up. She insisted, as I'd hoped she would, that I move into the flat, in spite of the inconvenience this would cause. A bed was put up for me on the couch in the living-room. Fenter, who kept his distance from me, did not object: not in my presence, at least.

The flat was on the second floor of a long slab of a building that looked out on an exact replica of itself on the other side of the street. Trams passed just below the living-room window; I used to sit there with Saskia, the older girl, and we would try to throw one-kirat coins on their roofs as they went by. Saskia loved the game. We counted it as a success only if the coin did not bounce off, but landed and stuck on the tram-roof; then Saskia would marvel to think of it being carried around the streets of the city forever. "Get ready!" she'd cry out in great excitement, every time a tram turned into the street, with a stiff, sudden sway of its entire body, almost like that of a woman wearing a bustle.

Sitting with Saskia, watching our coins drop and fly off in all directions, I remembered how I had listened with my mother, in this same city, to the noises the trams had made, and how they had amazed me with their variety. They were still at it – humming, thrumming, clicking, smacking, kissing, squeaking, grinding, slithering – as well as making certain other noises which can be conveyed only by words whose sound have no connection with their sense: dagger-dagger-dagger, for example, or an expiring and utterly gentle harsh-sh . . .

When Saskia was away at school, and Fenter was at work, I sat at the window on my own, and watched the housewives doing their chores in the flats across the street. Beata never disturbed me. Then my mother would come round the corner, and I would lean further forward to look at her making her way, finger trailing behind her, towards us.

On the third or fourth day after my arrival I went on the inevitable pilgrimage to Vliss. I don't know what I expected to get out of the trip: certainly not a feeling of sheer relief at realising that I would never again have any conceivable occasion to visit the place. It was finished. Finished the unpaved track, whose very stones were familiar to me, leading to the schoolhouse; finished the store where my father had worked; finished this fence, that shed, the station. The lot. I went into Pieck's bar, which now had a new name and a new owner, and drank a few beers. Through the open window I could see what had once been my mother's shop, just discernible among the huddled buildings on the far side of the square. Only then did it occur to me that the past was not a realm to which the laws of perspective applied in any way. Nearer and farther had no meaning within it. In a room above that shop I had sat on my father's lap, feeling his secret warmth beneath me, breathing in his mealy, manly odour, wondering how each black, curling hair of his moustache could be endowed with a mysterious life of its own. But the fact that I had such a memory of my father, and none of the Pharaohs of Egypt, meant nothing now to any of them. They were all equidistant from me; sealed together.

We like to talk bravely of our lives as a journey forward into the future. But we are whirled one way only, all of us. Backwards, into a dimensionless past.

Mr Kitzinger was dead too.

Then I returned to Boschoff, across the bald plain, with its dry, meandering gullies and silvery mirages shimmering above the road. Beata was pleased to find me looking more cheerful than when I had set out. "I thought it might depress you," she said, though she had encouraged me to make the journey.

"Why should it?" I answered. "Hell, to know I'll never have to go there again –!"

That night I celebrated my final release or discharge from Vliss by going with Fenter to a meeting of a club he belonged to. The Convivials, they called themselves. A sudden change of scene. I see myself sitting among the Convivials, at a table covered with a white cloth, in a room above a restaurant in town. I have already been formally introduced to everyone present, beginning of course with the chairman. Schlossberg is his name. He is an optician, and wears heavy spectacles on his nose, as if to advertise his trade. He has big hands and a solemn manner of speech, very suitable for a chairman. Because of his profession he evidently considers himself to be a man of science; because of his attachment to the opera, a man of culture. Next to him is Perrien, the treasurer, a dry, fanatic annotator of any piece of paper put in front of him, who works as an accountant in the Ministry of Pensions. Then Hilding, bonhomous, loud-laughing, untrustworthy, not too scrupulous about washing his head of prematurely greying hair. Since he, like Fenter, is a sub-editor on one of the local papers, they are referred to as "our representatives of the Fourth Estate". They are also spoken of as "the Young Turks" of the club. Then Ehlers, a schoolteacher, with a smiling jackal face and a jackal's delicate mien. Mr Neff, the smallest man present, an asthmatic, equipped like so many of his tribe with pouter-pigeon chest and square shoulders carried somewhere near his ears. And several others: Preiss, F'n Staden, Burger, Theunissen, Haack, Smit. All dear friends and fellow-members of the Convivials. Such entertaining people.

We eat the food brought up from below by Artur and his wife, the restaurateurs, who smile and nod and rub their hands at us. The wine circulates, and our foreheads begin to shine. Hilding tells a story about a man, a woman, and a dog. He utters the final words in a woman's falsetto: "I knew it couldn't be you, because his tongue was longer and so was his –!" Over coffee we are called to order by the chairman. There is some business to attend to. His false teeth move about in his mouth between sentences. Election of new members. Programme for bi-annual ladies' night. ("She's no lady, she's my wife!" Roar of laughter. That irrepressible Hilding.) Dues in arrears. ("Perhaps a few words from our treasurer might be in order on this subject . . .") Message of loyal congratulations to the newly appointed Prefect of Boschoff. (This is as close as the Convivials come to mentioning the distressing events that have prevented them from meeting for many months past.) Any other business? Neff's opportunity to speak, which he does after a certain amount of whistling and struggling. Proposes further joint evenings with the Panamanians and the Honourable Society of Mendicants. Deferred for further consideration. Any other questions? Right, gentlemen, back to our pleasures.

We break up into smaller groups to play knapp or klavveryas. A bottle of brandy is produced by Artur. Some play earnestly, others are more interested in the drink. This is the hour when the Convivials apparently settle down to gossip; to abuse each other; to be fined for "uttering words offensive to the dignity of a fellow-member"; to make up again ceremoniously; sometimes, in a corner, to hear surprising confessions about wives, children, money. I am told confidentially by several members that tears have been shed at this time, faces have been slapped, resignations have been handed in and withdrawn.

This particular evening goes by without any moments of high drama, however. By the end of it Artur and his wife are plainly anxious for us to leave, and their boy has fallen asleep on a chair on the landing. Hilding is completely drunk: two stunned eyes peer rigidly forward from his disintegrating face, and he moves like a man held upright by invisible hands under his armpits. Several other members of the club are unsteadier on their feet than before and more emphatic in their gestures. Some singing has taken place and been suppressed. We part on the pavement outside the cafe, assuring each other that we have had a wonderful evening. Fenter and I find ourselves saddled with Hilding, whose arms dangle uselessly before him, and whose feet meet the ground at unexpected moments, like a man on a swaying deck. Foxy Ehlers, too, is with us. Since he lives not far from Fenter, and it is a pleasant night, we decide to walk home together. Hilding says that he will do the same, though we doubt if he will be able to make it. He insists. We accede. Once outside the cafe, he falls into a melancholy silence, interrupted only by the occasional self-pitying hiccup. Ehlers and I talk cautiously about the news of the

137

day. We agree that we may now look forward "to a more settled period". Fenter, who has become more and more silent as the evening wears on, walks alongside us, making no contribution to the conversation. The jaunty, rather forced high spirits with which he set out from the flat have vanished – forever, one might suppose, looking at the scowl now fixed on his forehead.

When we were alone at last – Hilding having been abandoned on a bench, left sprawling anyhow on it; and Ehlers having let himself into his building with many cunning nods of farewell – Fenter wasted no time in giving vent to his feelings.

"Bastards! Cunts! Idiots! Creeps! Shits!"

"That's a funny way to talk about your friends," I replied, mildly enough.

"They're not my friends. I've got no friends."

His hands went deeper into his pockets, he pushed his head further forward, and increased the length of his stride. Each time we passed a lamp-post our shadows scooted ahead of us; then they became fainter and longer; then they vanished entirely, only to reappear behind us. And so to the next lamp-post; and the one after it. Apartment blocks stood shoulder to shoulder along the street, muffled lights burning within each ornate entry. No one else was in the street. No cars moved down it.

Eventually Fenter turned on me. "And you? What brings you here? All your big-shot friends finished – is that it? Cleaned out?"

"Pretty much."

"Serves them right."

"I think so too."

"They should shoot the bastards. Kill the whole lot of them."

"Perhaps."

"But you worked for them."

"Sure."

"Shit!"

I didn't know whether he was referring to my character in general or just to my last words.

"What are you going to do, then?"

"I'll find something."

"No doubt you will!"

He came to a halt, his eyes gleaming, his shadowy mouth puckered. Without warning he announced, "I've got another woman, you know."

I looked at him. His eyes seemed to feed on all the grains of light that swarmed between us. I waited for him to say more, but he neither spoke nor shifted his gaze.

"Why do you tell me?"

It took him a long time to reply.

"To stop you gloating."

"Gloating?"

"I know what you think. You think I've got a shitty little sub-editing job – and three kids – and debts – and your Beata! And I'm a member of the Convivials." He smiled with morose satisfaction. "Well, that's not all I've got."

"Does Beata know?"

"No."

"Are you going to tell her?"

"She's got kids too." It took me a moment to realise that he wasn't talking about Beata, but about his woman. "When she gets things sorted out, I'll tell Beata. Then she'll have to know. We're going to live together – me and –" He gestured across his body, towards the centre of town.

"What if I tell Beata?"

"You can if you like. I don't care. It'll make no difference in the end."

"And the kids?"

"I've worried enough about them. I started worrying about them too early."

I knew what he was referring to. A few minutes later we reached the apartment, and crept in as silently as we could, in order not to wake the children. But one of the older girls called out; then the baby started up.

I had already noticed – how could I not? – Beata's air of bridling insistence that all was well around her domestic hearth;

her efforts to make out that her family was as happy and united as any to be seen on the posters for National Redemption Bonds. This had irritated me and roused my suspicions: now I found it simply pathetic to see her curveting flirtatiously between her husband and her children, while he scowled and shifted his tongue about in his cheeks, and the two older children, who were not to be fooled so easily, looked doubtfully at him. Yet the children wanted to believe in her enthusiasms almost as much as she did. So they made insincere exclamations of excitement and pleasure over nothing, and pretended not to hear when Daddy told Mommy to fuck off, he was tired, he didn't care to see her arsing about in front of him.

I said nothing to Beata about Fenter's announcement. There seemed no point in doing so while I remained uncertain about how to proceed. What I did do, though, was to find out who his new woman was. I wanted to laugh when I saw her. She was so like Beata! Tired, small, vulnerable, neatly shabby, timorously hopeful – she and Beata could have been sisters.

I had followed Fenter from his work-place; I saw them meet in the Plaas, where my mother and I had once waited during my father's trial; they sat on a bench and talked, before parting with a hurried kiss. I then followed her to a small, iron-roofed house with a scrap of neglected garden in front of it, a long distance out in the suburbs. By pretending to be an insurance salesman I got her name – Fermeulen, it was – from the snub-nosed boy who answered my knock. I was already at the gate by the time the woman came to the door.

The next day I was back in that district. But it wasn't Mef. Fermeulen who had brought me back there so promptly. While tailing her I had had some kind of recollection of a much earlier trek through that mean multiplicity of suburban streets. Nothing I had seen had been familiar to me, yet I had known exactly how the land rose and fell at every turn; I had recognised its rhythms, so to speak. How could this be? The sensation was so puzzling I came back determined to identify what was even less than a memory; rather, a kind of obscure striving for balance within me.

My search did not take long. I sat in the tram for a few stops beyond the point where Fenter's lady-love had got off; then, following my instinct, I climbed off, passed under a subway, walked down a long, straight street, with traffic-islands in the middle of it, adorned by dusty shrubs planted in the white-washed halves of old oil-drums; turned a corner . . . and there it was.

It hadn't changed at all. I knew that at once. I could mark off each feature as if on a register in my mind: tall fences of barbed-wire; the guardhouse at the gate within a clump of trees; gravelled roads leading to large and small stone buildings in the distance; identical barred windows, singly or in rows. Even the black shadows of the trees, motionless on the earth around the guard-house, seemed exactly as they had been when I had last come there, hand in hand with my mother. And the conical ventilators along the roof-crest of each big building: how could I ever have imagined that I had forgotten them?

I approached the gate. A guard in the door to the gatehouse noticed me and lumbered over to ask me what I wanted. I told him, the words jumping out of my mouth, that I was interested in joining the prison service.

He looked humorously at me, from under his peaked cap. His red face seemed to ooze indiscriminately over its own features. "You don't want to do that."

"What do you mean?"

Only after I'd spoken did I realise he wasn't accusing me of being a liar; he was merely flippantly offering me some advice. He hitched up his uniform trousers over his stomach, unsuccess-fully. "The pay's terrible. And the company –!" He hawked elaborately, turned his head aside, and spat on the ground. The blob of spittle instantly became a ball of dust.

"No – seriously," I said.

"I am serious."

"Well, how did *you* join?" I challenged him.

"My father worked here."

"So did mine."

"Then you should know the ropes."

"He didn't stick it long."

"What makes you think you'd like it better?"

"I don't know, I thought I might try."

"You go to the police station. They got the forms."

I walked on. He watched me go. That very next morning I followed his instructions and got the set of forms from a police station. But when I looked at the questions on them I decided it would be too risky to fill them in. Another career gone for good! Or so I thought.

A few days later I met Dafne Mainckies. Years before, in the church-hall in Vliss, I had seen her as a shadowy, magical creature of flickering black and silver, constantly changing size, constantly approaching and receding from me, while her muffled voice came from a box on the floor nearby. She had embraced her lovers before my eyes, pressing long fingers into their shoulders; she had cried silently at the graveside of her illegitimate child; she had run down a hillside to greet her father back from the wars; she had died heroically, under torture, refusing to give away the secrets of the Phalanx in revolutionary days. Whereupon, when the curtains in the hall were opened, and the lights came on again, I had spent hours wandering about the fields and lanes of the village, dreaming of a life devoted to her service.

Now my dreams had come true.

XVII

FROM THEN ON my luck changed, and I began the climb that was to bring me – here. To this little village in the mountains, where I have come ostensibly for a spell of "rest and reflection", before taking up the new duties publicly assigned to me by the Heerser.

It would be quite false, as I shall soon show, to imagine that I enjoyed an unbroken ascent to this literal and metaphorical height. Yet I can truthfully say that even at the jerkiest or most haphazard moments of my progress, and even though I never knew what my ultimate destination might be, I felt that I was indeed progressing; I was moving in the right direction. My confidence was not merely the result of successive strokes of good fortune; it was positively a guarantee that they would continue to come my way.

The explanation was not far to seek. The simultaneous discovery and dismissal of one preposterous hope – the hope of escape or reformation, which some part of myself had been secretly nourishing for so long – had generated another, rarer kind of hope, indistinguishable from resignation. Even the anguish I had felt about the discovery had contained within it the seeds of a new-found self-assurance. I knew where I was. I could relax. I no longer expected transformations. Therefore, transformations of another kind were granted to me.

For instance: what a long time it had taken me to realise I

could never possibly succeed in those branches of the service to which my instinct for betrayal had almost automatically attracted me! The Compresecor, for example. I was quite unfitted for a conventional career in such an organisation. The reason is so obvious it embarrasses me to have to present it, at this stage, as a great, belated discovery. To be really successful in an agency of that kind you had to care nothing about those you used and destroyed on your way up. Lingering loyalties, obsessional tender-nesses and cruelties, gratuitous betrayals and curiosities of the kind so necessary to me, were not merely a disadvantage; they were radically disabling. Destroy and wash your hands; break and forget – that was the way ahead for your wholehearted careerist. I couldn't do it. I loved my victims. I was unable to let them go. I gripped them as tightly as my own passions gripped me. That was why I had pursued Fenter into marrying my sister; why Gita and I were still lovers, and Serle and I still friends; there was nothing accidental about it. It wasn't their doing, as I had liked to imagine, but mine. Always mine.

So I had to find some other way forward. (I am telling the story from the vantage-point of knowing its end, of course: not as it appeared to me then, as I groped through the mists and congeal-ments of an uncomprehended present.) I was an expert in betrayal? An expert in love? Only those whom I betrayed I loved? Well then –

Well then – get on with it. Time runs out. Picture me a few years later, a married man, the stepfather of two children, the owner of an apartment in a pleasant quarter of Port Margriet.

It was an old apartment, but a large and comfortable one. From the balcony just outside the living-room there was a view, of which I was particularly proud, across the city to the lake and the mountains on both sides of it. At all seasons the mountains were almost as variable in hue and texture as the water; sometimes in winter they disappeared entirely and a mist filled the streets below, while invisible ships blurted out their sorrows over the entire city.

At such times I relished all the more the comforts within. My study, first on the left. The dining-room. The living-room. The main bedroom. The children's bedrooms. Wallpapers throughout beige in colour and dimpled like seersucker. Glass lampshades cut to resemble tulips sticking out of the walls. Upholstered arm-chairs in the living-room bulging within cloth covers like so many heavily corseted women. On the walls pictures in gilt frames of traditional subjects – fruit and flowers tumbling out of urns onto comatose rabbits; ladies of Egyptian appearance looking out upon the construction of pyramids; peasant lads and lasses sporting among stooks of hay. Immediately outside was a landing encased in pale, coffin-like, polished wood; downstairs were the modest splendours of the foyer, all marble and tarnished nickel.

The total effect? (My choice, I may say, not my wife's; she submitted to me in the matter of decor, as in every other.) Solid, respectable, conventional, more than a little dull. Suitable for a minor civil servant, say. A shopkeeper. A schoolmaster, possibly. A man of restrained ambitions and pretensions. Who retires to his study every evening, more for the sake of impressing his wife than to do any work. Who smokes a cigar or two after dinner. Who might even be a member of a club composed of people like himself, which meets once a month above a restaurant in town. Who pays his dues willingly to the Phalanx; goes to chapel regularly; listens with much attention to certain favourite radio programmes; performs his exercises on rising each morning; and reads the more serious of the two dailies published in town.

Some of these guesses would be right; some wrong. Before going any further with these interesting matters, however, do allow me to introduce you to my wife.

But of course! How forgetful of me! You have met before. You met her when she was married to the late Advocate-General Haifert.

What a tragic business that was! But as you see, out of such tragedies good does sometimes come. Trude and the two dear children have been able to make a new life for themselves, thank God, and I've been lucky enough to be in a position to help them do so . . .

No wonder I wear such a complacent expression on my face as I bring her forward. No wonder she is so hurried and severe in her manner. In spite of all the time we have spent together she never relaxes, poor thing. (Not even, I may say in strict confidence, when her hips and thighs heave and plunge beneath me, while her open palms hold me delicately, one on each side of my naked rib-cage, as if grasping a precious, fragile object which has only just come into her possession.) And no wonder the children fawn on me when they come home from school, and cling to my hands, and even kiss them furtively. I am associated in their minds with the most frightening passage in their lives; therefore they can afford to take no risks with me.

Happy household scenes. I had discovered yet another secret vice: domesticity. Domesticity on these terms, I mean. Domesticity licensed by fear and secrecy. Bringing itself up for incredulous examination and self-questioning in the small hours of every night. Whose every pleasure has a shadow of guilt and every passion a core of self-hatred. Whose past is full of shame and suspicion and whose future is – more of the same. Domesticity *à la* Josef Baisz, in short.

But it suited her too. It wasn't just that my obsessions had been stronger than her powers of resistance. She had obsessions of her own. As a husband I offered her a kind of revenge: not so much against me as against life in general. I had been the kidnapper of her children. The murderer (in a sense) of her husband. The destroyer of her home. These facts made a relationship impossible in her eyes. In mine they made it imperative. An extraordinary intimacy existed between us as a result.

Of course, a formal, daylight version of the catastrophic events in which we had been jointly involved had been agreed between us. A grand but entirely honourable passion for her had burned in my breast from the moment I had entered her house. Later "they" (the Compresecor) had said that they would kill my sister and her husband if I did not cooperate with them. I had driven to the farmhouse at the point of crazy Anton's pistol. Once there I had schemed day and night how I might escape, with the children. My plan had miscarried. As a hunted man, I had been unable to get back to them. Fortunately Anton had simply abandoned them, after an interval whose length it was now impossible to establish, and they had made their way to the main road and begged help from a passing motorist.

But they had returned too late to save their father. Though he had left no note, it was obvious he had hoped that once he was out of the way the Compresecor would have no more use for them, and would let them go. Perhaps, too, he had wanted to warn his fellow-conspirators that they were in trouble. So he had gone into his study and heroically put a bullet through his head.

Clearly, no later love could erase the place he occupied in her heart; and I, who had also revered the Advocate-General, would not wish it otherwise.

But whether, as he took his gun out of the drawer of his desk, he had believed in the veracity and weight of what he was doing; whether he was condemned even then to be spectator as well as performer of his own action; whether in the last, infinitesimal moment of consciousness granted to him he had cried out un-availingly to the producer or playwright in his own mind, No, no! – on none of these points were Trude and I able to enlighten one another. Lying alongside her at night I could only guess at the answers to these questions – lingeringly, lovingly, gloatingly if you like; but with a depth of shared feeling that does not surprise me in the least, whatever it might do to more naive or optimistic moralists.

Was ever woman in such fashion woo'd? asks Shakespeare's Richard III, pursuing a widow whom he himself had widowed. I am in a position to recommend the fashion to others. It gave ferocity to our matrimonial embraces. It filled with anxiety the glances we exchanged across the domestic dinner-table. It charged our silences with an intensity they wouldn't otherwise have had. It enabled me to feel a more than stepfatherly tenderness towards the children. For Trude it was a never-failing source of astonishment.

Anything was possible: that was what she had learned from me.

Or so she believed. She actually said so, shortly after we had begun to see one another again, and I had made clear my intentions towards her. "Yes," I answered. "You just have to be prepared to imagine it – whatever you like –"

"Then you're free!" she exclaimed.

Was I to disillusion her? To tell her that the imagination of evil could be as constricting, as repetitive, as jealous a taskmaster, as any god of puritan morality?

I did no such thing. I kept silent.

"You see, I'm not afraid," she went on. "Not any more. How can I be, after all that's happened?"

I took her by the waist. When I put my lips to hers I heard her hiss like a goose: whether in despair or lust, I could not tell. Her hip-bones writhed against mine. Our first kiss.

Almost immediately she broke away from me. But the next words she uttered revealed to me how close I was to winning her. She said disconsolately, averting her face with all the pathos of a woman's common-place vanity, "I'm so much older than you are."

She was an admirable wife. Let me pay her that tribute whole-heartedly. The efficiency I had resented as a servant appeared in quite a different light once I had become her husband. Her restraint also acquired a new value after I became its beneficiary, so to speak, rather than its victim. She did not ask for more information on any topic than I was prepared to give her. Because of our circumstances we had few acquaintances in the city. It might be said that we lived an austere, reserved, even secretive life. She had met none of the members of my family, and I had met almost none of hers. Her mother was the exception: a dour, suspicious widow, whom we had left behind in Bailaburg.

We had agreed that we would not start a family of our own. Perhaps later it might be possible. But not now.

XVIII

No, I HAVEN'T FORGOTTEN about Dafne Mainckies. For reasons which will become obvious, I have merely postponed the painful task of speaking about what happened while I was in her employ. But I can put off that part of the story no longer.

Besides, it would be particularly poor recompense for me to pretend to have forgotten Dafne, when she had remembered me so well. Our first meeting had taken place while I had been guarding the body of Professor Watermaier. She had been one of the mourners in the room when the corpse had been snatched from under my nose. I had even spoken to her, without knowing who she was, just before I'd run out of the house and emptied my pistol at the retreating hearse. But, strange as it seemed to me, she hadn't regarded me simply as a fool and a dupe. Not at all. She had been struck by my decisiveness and fidelity to the job in hand. Also by my ruthlessness. So she took me on with alacrity when I turned up amongst those who replied to her advertisement in the columns of the *Boschoff Courant*.

Absurd, isn't it? I did not tell her what I thought of that wretched episode. Or what my superiors had said about it. Then and later I merely looked modest when she spoke of it.

We met in the sitting-room of her suite in Boschoff's oldest and best hotel. There were flowers in vases; glass-topped, half-moon tables against the walls, with gilded legs that tapered down to

149

dog-like claws; mirrors that reflected bits of floral carpet and white shutters. She sat in one armchair; I in another. Now that I knew who she was I marvelled equally at how like and how unlike she was to the fantasy figure of my boyhood. She was much older, of course; larger, broader, longer in the leg, bolder in the eye, more strongly moulded in the face; more copious altogether. Strangely, the screen had had a moderating, refining effect on her appearance, all those close-ups notwithstanding. At first I found it difficult to attend to what she was saying; I was too busy with my own suddenly rediscovered memories of her. That pause before giving emphasis to the last word of a sentence, with her lips moving almost imperceptibly forward before she uttered it – how uncannily intimate it was; and how implausible just for that reason! At one moment she looked like a handsome, reserved, dignified, middle-aged lady who had never known anything but the pleasures and austerities of private life; the next, like Dafne Mainckies earnestly playing such a role.

She was dressed in a loose, silken dress of black material with white flowers printed upon it; it had large sleeves that fell back from her arms. Her face was carefully made up: powder, a faint lipstick, eye-shadow on the lids of her famous, violet eyes. Her brows looked untouched by pencil or tweezers; her grey hair hung loosely, youthfully, in a thick, simple cut, down to her shoulders. She made no attempt to charm me. She was in fact brusque, nervous, rather shy. Only when I had accepted her offer, and we had agreed on the details of the appointment, did she smile for the first time. Her lips grew thinner, her chin longer. Her eyes rested on me gravely and watchfully. Yet that look was part of the smile, too. Then she stood up to see me to the door. She was tall; her stride was mannish; so were her shoulders.

"I am glad we've come to an understanding," she said, at the door. "I do feel you're someone I can trust."

Our eyes met. We shook hands. She was very much the grand lady; but how vulnerable she was, at the same time; how much in need of succour.

It was an impeccable performance: if it was a performance.

What do you do if, having once been a famous figure on our cinema screens, your pride forbids you to dwindle into an old woman playing interesting "character" parts in films of which others are the stars? If the single attempt you made to become a stage-actress, appearing in the classical, passion-torn, older roles (Cleopatra, Phaedra, our own Magda f'n Zail), was not judged a success? If you are rich, well regarded on the highest levels of party and state, and admired unbegrudgingly in artistic circles precisely because you no longer appear to be a contender for honours? If you have energy and presence; looks as well preserved as you can expect them to be at your age; influential friends; a house in the hills above the Lecke Lake; a personal assistant who adores you, and a maid, ditto?

Most of these questions are fairly easy to answer. You become chairman of the State Film Investment Corporation: a well-funded body set up jointly by the Ministry of Light Industry and the Ministry of National Guidance to foster film-making in general and to finance particular productions. You become the mistress of our old friend, His Honour Maximilian Spass, formerly deputy Prime Minister, now promoted, as a result of many wise decisions on difficult occasions, to membership of the party's Directorate, of which he is First Treasurer. You take long holidays, usually in your house in the country, sometimes in the houses of your friends, and occasionally abroad. You sit on the management committees of the National Theatre, the Heddesen Memorial School of Drama, the Youth Propaganda Theatre Group, and the Retired Actors' Pension Fund. You make occasional broadcasts and appear as an honoured guest at many public functions. You patronise young artists who paint your portrait, and young writers who dedicate their poems to you. You collect silver and china. You give parties which are attended by celebrities and grandees of all kinds. You watch closely over successive re-releases of your old films, making sure that they are not tampered with and that you receive your proper share of the proceeds.

In short, you keep yourself busy. Your diary is always full.

Martha Krause, your personal assistant, always has a great deal of work to do, none of which she begrudges you. Short neck tilted forward, well-padded shoulders curved in upon themselves – so that her forequarters appear to have been manufactured out of a single piece of thick rubber – she wears on your behalf, especially around her pug mouth, an expression of neurotic determination. Her time is always at your disposal. So is that of Bettina, your maid. Bettina doesn't merely live in, but apparently never goes out; she blinks her colourless eyelids at the very thought of it.

Everything revolves around you, then, in orderly and peaceful fashion. Your long-standing affair with the First Treasurer is conducted with an old-fashioned discretion and decorum on both sides. His wife has agreed to give you no trouble as long as you don't make a fool of her, as she has vulgarly put it; and the First Treasurer is anxious to oblige her, for he knows how puritanical the Heerser is in sexual matters. *He* will absent-mindedly slip his hand into the tunic of a member of the Palace Guard, and squeeze one of the nipples he finds there until tears of pain and mortification stand in the guardsman's eyes; but he does not like sexual scandal of any kind to attach itself to the people who hold posts immediately beneath him. So Spass seldom spends the night at your house in town; instead you meet each other at the houses of friends or he visits you in the country. As might be expected of mature people, you both accept without resentment these limitations on your freedom, and do not repine for what you cannot have.

But (*why* must there always be a "but"?) there is a flaw or breach in your life which you cannot mend, a source of pain you cannot cure. It is your only son, Ritchie. About the loss of much of your beauty and fame, about your lover, your career, your finances, you have done everything that prudence and self-knowledge would advise. About Ritchie it seems that there is nothing you can do. You have tried pleas, tears, anger, indifference; private tutors, psychiatrists, pastors, boarding schools, a military gymnasium, an institution for disturbed children, special therapeutic work-camps; you have even hired girls to live in the house, in the hope that one or another of them might take the responsibility for him off your shoulders.

Wasted efforts, all of them. He has no job and will not look for one. He wears filthy clothes. He lies in bed for days on end. He insults Martha, Bettina, and all your friends. His worst insults, however, he saves for the First Treasurer, and for the liaison between the two of you. He cries often. He has tried to dig up his father's grave in order to prove that he was not killed in a motor accident, as the official story goes, but was poisoned by your lover, with your connivance. He has ridden a motor-bike up the steps of the Stockdaal Theatre, when you were attending an opening night there. He has been arrested twice: the first time for possessing drugs, the second for shoplifting. (On both occasions he was released quietly after intercession by the First Treasurer.) He has no friends; no hobbies; no skills; apparently no interests, except in tormenting you.

This is the son who phones you up, while you are on a three-week visit to Boschoff on Film Corporation business, to announce that he's got into trouble with some people he knows. He can't tell you on the phone what kind of trouble it is; but it's serious, the worst trouble he's ever been in, a matter of life and death. So he's going to "hide out" in your cottage in Wesselt until "the thing has blown over". On no account is anyone to be told where he's gone.

His voice breaks, he sobs, and rings off. Again! How can you tell what the trouble is this time, or if it is as bad as he says? What you do know for certain is that he is pathetic and infuriating, depressing and contemptible, a weight on a mother's heart. And so boring!

Then: a brainwave. Hitherto almost all your efforts have been directed towards trying to reclaim him from above, as it were, by providing him with wise counsellors, moral exemplars, understanding therapists. But perhaps what he really needs is someone more like himself; not at all like the ambitious, artistic, creditable young man you once hoped he might become. Perhaps he needs somebody tough, cynical, unscrupulous if necessary, physically strong, not afraid of taking risks, who can win his respect at the only level at which he might be capable of feeling respect, and thus be able to control him and keep him out of mischief. You happen to be in Boschoff, a relatively strange town. The case is urgent. There is nothing to stop you advertising in the local paper, like any other citizen in need, stating in the most guarded terms what you are looking for. The truth can come later, once you have found a suitable applicant.

Then you will go straight to the cottage in Wesselt with this new member of your entourage, this bodyguard/keeper/companion. Ritchie is not to know why he has been hired: he will be presented merely as your new driver and helper. Thereafter you will leave the two of them to their own devices, and hope for the best.

But to what extent in these schemes and daydreams you are driven by love for your son, by the desire to rid yourself of a nuisance, by disappointment in him, even by a desire for revenge against him – this you do not know yourself. Nor does your hired man. Nor will he ever know.

What he can tell you, however, is that his heart contracted with a strange pleasure and fear the moment he saw your son. Indeed, he can remember the very words that passed through his mind, as your car halted in front of the cottage and Ritchie came out of the door to greet you.

This time, he thought, I've found a winner.

XIX

REMEMBERING THAT FIRST SIGHT OF HIM, I now have to restrain myself from rushing forward to the moment of laborious cruelty, of mechanical terror, when my appointment as his keeper came to its end. Why the hurry? Because hindsight still has its noose tight around my neck. It cannot wait to remind me of how heavily I moved on that narrow cliffside ledge, high up on the Enckelberg – like an automaton, a man performing a grotesque chore. How can hindsight forgo such a chance to play the great moraliser; to wag its head at me and speak reprovingly of its favourite subjects: of compassion, and of remorse, and of honour?

Fine words! But I won't have it lecturing to me: not on those grounds, at any rate. Compassion? I know all about compassion. It's one of my specialities. If we can feel pain at the suffering of our fellows, then we are ineluctably endowed with the potentiality of taking pleasure in it too. There is no getting round it. If I had not been devoured by a longing to share the experience of others, indeed to amalgamate it with my own, Ritchie Mainckies would never have meant anything to me. Honour? The same! It was because I was compelled to prove myself worthy of my own fantasies and of the expectations of others, like any real man of honour, that I acted as I did on that mountainside. As for remorse – nothing, in my experience, so hardens the heart as the prospect or threat of remorse. Quite rightly! What is the reward for submitting to it, after all? More remorse! Keener remorse! Thank you very much. Better by far to deny, for as long as you possibly can, like every other villain, that you have ever done anything to occasion it.

It amazes me how these moral concepts are bandied about, in such a simple-minded fashion, as if nothing but good can flow from them; as if there is not another, darker side welded logically to each of them. Necessarily welded to them. Eternally welded to them.

Ritchie. I left him standing on the top step of the verandah. Looking back I find it difficult to understand why I was so certain he would be a zealous, even grateful partner to me; a fit subject for the exercise of power and perfidy. If I try to exclude from my memory all extraneous sights and sounds – the sprawling house, with its curious appearance of leaning back from the white-pillared verandah before it; Dafne's cry of greeting; the sway of ilex leaves above the car, halted in the little driveway – if I exclude these and stare through lapsed, unalterable time and dead event at the slightly built youth in shirtsleeves standing above us, I am left with two impressions which now seem inconsequential or even absurd, and yet appeared quite conclusive at the time. The first was his wraith-like, veering, swaying manner of carrying his head and shoulders, like someone with smoke inside him instead of flesh and blood. The second was his moustache. Ridiculously out of proportion for a face as small and youthful as the one it rested on, it was a blond, cascading affair, of a kind that might have been expected to adorn the mouth of a crazy nineteenth-century philosopher. Above this implausibly ferocious growth was a pair of weak brown eyes, full of wonder and reflection, and a head of hair the colour of dry maize-stalks. It looked almost as if it might crackle were you to run your hand over it. The uncombed back of his head was so boyish and so earnest in appearance it seemed a wholly suitable container for the confusion and exaltation I was to discover within.

Then there were his lips. His lower lip, at least. I noticed it late, because his moustache was so overbearing; when I did, I was surprised by its pinkness, and by how far forward it was thrust; and with what a pertinacious air. In the days and weeks that followed I was to read his thoughts as much by the movements of that lip as by any other change in his features. I got to know every angle at which it came to rest, its movements when he spoke, the fierce sudden appearances it made when he ate.

In the first flurry of arrival he did no more than nod at me. His mother he kissed; Martha Krause, who had accompanied us on the long drive from Boschoff, he favoured with a scowl. I took up the ladies' bags, and was then shown to my little bedroom on the first floor, at the end of a long passage. The house was a rambling place on many levels, or half-levels, amply furnished with old, simple, and what I judged to be expensive stuff: polished wooden bedsteads and chests in the bedrooms; chintz-covered armchairs and settees in the living-room; roll-top desks and a variety of bookcases in Dafne's study; damp-patched prints on the walls; brass, pewter, and hand-painted china everywhere. There was a garden and drive in front, and a lawn at the back which sloped down to a pond where some ducklings and their mother sailed the water together. All round were fields and orchards and woods; farther off, the omnipresent mountains, the thin covering of trees on their flanks broken only by outcrops of rock. Their colours were always changing; their distant gaze always seemed to be directed at one another, never at us. Wesselt village was a few kilometres away; from a group of houses nearby there came the girl who swept and cooked, and her father who cut the grass and grew vegetables in a patch to the side of the house.

What had Ritchie been doing before our arrival? He wouldn't say at first. Later it emerged he'd been "writing", among other things. But mostly he'd just been "lying low". "Keeping under cover." "Taking no chances." When I asked him to tell me exactly why he was in hiding, or from whom he was hiding, his answers were vague and evasive. However, I did eventually manage to get a fairly coherent story out of him. He had fallen in with some professional gamblers in Bailaburg, played for high stakes, lost, and then forged his mother's signature to a cheque for several thousand kirats in payment of his debts to them. The cheque would bounce, must already have bounced, the gamblers would be after him, his mother still had to learn what he had done to her.

"Lucky you've got me," I said, and drew my pistol out of my pocket.

It fascinated him, as I already knew by then. He stared sombrely at it, as if mesmerised by it: by its flatness and blackness; its imperfect parallelogram of a butt, angled to the rest and scored with cross-hatching; its ever-open mouth, rounded in an expression of imbecile willingness. Overhanging the butt, like the back of a tiny cranium, was the curve of metal that contained the firing mechanism: the only brain it had, capable of performing just one trick. I weighed it, holding it out before Ritchie, while his lower lip moved, uncertain what words to form. Before he could make up his mind I put the gun away.

We were walking across the field immediately behind the house. It sloped down to some woodland; then the climb to the mountains began. In the middle of the field we came upon the contracted, dried-out carcass of a jackal, curled up on its side. Some rusty fur was left on what had been its legs and back; out of its clenched jaw a chicken-bone pointed directly skyward, like a marker or compass-needle. We knew the story of that jackal. It had been stealing poultry from the farms all round. So a neighbour had put out a chicken shot full of strychnine, which the beast had taken. It had died on the spot; then its carcass had been left as a bait for others. Ritchie and I stopped to stare at it. We had stopped there before. There were no flies or maggots on it; not now, at any rate.

He asked, "When are you going to let me have another go with the gun?"

"One of these days."

"One of these days!" He imitated me unpleasantly, trying to take off a northern accent. "One of those weeks. One of these years."

"It could be," I said. "It's up to you."

"If I'm a good boy?"

"Exactly."

"Shit on you!"

But he didn't leave me. We walked on together. It was a wind-less, close day: the clouds were low overhead and shone as if burdened with heat rather than moisture. We were both in our shirtsleeves; I could smell my own sweat. At last we came to the shade of the woodland. A little stream trickled through it, from one scum-laden pool to the next. Above each pool the air was tremulous with darting, hovering insect-life. I sat on a fallen tree-trunk; Ritchie lay on his back, on the grass. Then he moved to put the heel of one foot on my thigh. The foot stuck up in front of me. I let it remain there. His eyes were closed. His breast rose and fell.

That was how far we had got within a few days of my arrival. It had been easier than I had expected to win his confidence. All I had had to do initially was to betray his mother's. She had wanted to hide the fact that I was hired primarily to look after him; her idea had been that I should make myself indispensable to him without rousing his suspicion that that was precisely what she had intended all along. By telling Ritchie immediately about her scheme I had persuaded him that we could be friends, allies, in league against her; that she was the one who was being made a fool of, not him.

The next step, also taken almost immediately, had been to offer to teach him how to handle my gun. The last was to hit him.

I doubt if anyone in a position of authority had ever hit him before. Not hard, anyway. He was greatly impressed by the experience: incredulous at first, then angry, then reflective, then affectionate. It happened when I came into my room one morning and found him going through my meagre possessions. Almost instinctively I reached out and slapped him. He stood by an open drawer, staring at me, not trying to defend himself. So I hit him again with my open palm, backhand and forehand, coming and going as it were. I felt the resilience of his nose and lips against the back of my hand; underneath was the hard bone. Wetness too. His face suddenly became all tears and snot, pallor and redness, with his moustache projecting stupidly from it. We were both panting. I lifted my hand again. This time he lowered his head and scuttled past me. I let him go.

When I asked him later what he had been looking for, he answered simply, "I thought you might have another gun."

From then on we were like lovers. I use the word circumspectly, knowing how it will be interpreted, but also without misgiving. The nearest we ever came to being lovers physically was – well, not very near: we once sat for a long time silently, hand in hand, in a darkened room. We never used any endearments in speaking to each other. But we were like lovers in the exclusivity of our relationship: we constantly sought each other out and valued our exchanges with outsiders, Dafne included, only so far as they could later be a subject for comment and reflection between us.

Days passed. So full while we lived through them, they flaked away and lay behind us, without dimension, taking up no space once they were past. The same ever-recurring, age-old deceit! We indulged in lacerating bouts of merriment over trivialities. We imitated Dafne doing her exercises (in trousers and a black top) out on the lawn. We went into the mountains and practised shooting at targets with my pistol. I passed on to him all the tricks of the bodyguarding trade which I had learned in Burzenack. I tailed him through the streets of Port Margriet – the two of us having specially driven down there for the day – and let him do the same to me: the one who went longest without his quarry spotting him was the "winner". I told him stories from my large store of real and imaginary adventures as a bodyguard. I listened to his views on God and the meaning of life, and the vileness of the Phalanx for Democratic Control, and the special vileness of Max Spass. I agreed with these views. I praised him. I abused his mother. I promised to take revenge on all his enemies. I promised him fame. I promised him power. Assured him he was marked out for a singular fate. Speculated with him about how he might win fame: as a great writer, a great criminal, a great revolutionary, a great hypnotist. Swore to him that together we would give them all the zu-zu-zap.

This last plagiarism was an instant success, by the way. The accompanying gesture too. He used it frequently on his mother, whose spectacular eyes widened with conscientious good humour every time she heard it.

Martha Krause had returned to the capital after only a few days; we three stayed on. Nothing had been heard from Dafne's bank about the forged cheque; so complete had the silence been on the subject that I'd begun to wonder if the whole story hadn't been a fabrication, or at any rate a great exaggeration, which Ritchie himself had come to believe in. But I said no more about it to him, and had not mentioned it at all to his mother. For her part, she left us alone, pleased with the progress I seemed to be making. When she wasn't gardening (in a big straw hat), or cooking (in a brief apron), or doing her exercises (as described), she kept herself busy with her many friends who were holidaying in cottages like her own in the neighbourhood. Among these were writers, actors, producers, some eminent academics, a few politicians and high government officials mixing during their vacations in what they considered to be interestingly Bohemian circles. Professor Andrie, the boss of my former boss, Serle, figured among them too: he had managed to retire peacefully from his position as Minister of National Guidance, and still had his head of white hair quite intact. He did not recognise me, of course, and I did not remind him who I was.

On the whole these people had done very well out of the regime; yet they prided themselves, I noticed, on the independence of their views and the frankness with which they expressed them. They weren't going to swallow "all that stuff" which their new chum, Professor Andrie, had once put out; they were different, set apart from the mass. Thus – to give just one example of what I mean – Dafne Mainckies, she of the violet eyes and famous profile, head of the State Film Corporation and mistress of Max Spass, had found it quite easy to become a friend of the late, refractory Professor Hans Watermaier. Ritchie used to entertain me with descriptions of their meetings: she sitting (metaphorically) at his feet, drinking in his wisdom; his eyes rummaging about, as far as they could get, inside her blouse or up her skirt . . . At which point Ritchie's own eyes would begin to roll and his voice would thicken. "Fucking hypocrite! Old goat! Bloody Water-Maker!"

XX

THE BOY WAS HALF-CRAZY to begin with, you understand.

That he adored his mother; that he hated and resented her precisely because he adored her; that he was rabidly jealous of her; that he transmuted his jealousy into a loathing of "society" or "the regime" for their cruelty, hypocrisy, corruption, etc, etc – all this is banal, obvious, predictable. What is more (and here we come to something much less predictable) Ritchie knew it. Knowing it inflamed him and enraged him all the more. It filled him with ambition to prove that he was special, singular, not predictable at all. Particularly after I had turned up, with my gun and my stories and my quasi-paternal interest in him. Even my father's fate, of which I did not fail to tell him, became in his eyes yet another example of the oppression of the humble people of the Republic by their rulers. His mother's lover was of course numbered among those rulers.

But let me make it clear now rather than later that I did not urge Ritchie Mainckies to make an attempt on the life of First Treasurer Spass.

So far I have tried to tell the truth. I intend to carry on doing so. No-one can accuse me of glossing over my actions or of trying to find excuses for them. The only justification I sought for my deeds was the pleasure they gave me. That was sufficient. It still has to be. I use the word "pleasure" to cover many emotions, of course: terror and love among them. Perhaps I should speak of intensity, rather. Let that convey what I mean. What I valued above all other ends. And still seek now, in the very act of putting down the word, in these circumstances.

After all of which I repeat: I didn't encourage Ritchie to attack Spass. On the contrary. All I did was to tell him that he would never do any such thing. That he was incapable of it. That I didn't want to listen to his fantasies on the subject. That I despised him for indulging in them.

It was enough. His honour was also at stake, after all.

I can remember clearly the first time I heard him utter a direct threat against Spass, as distinct from general, aimless abuse of him. We had eaten at a table on the lawn, the three of us, as we often did in the evenings. The meal had gone off peacefully enough. Dafne had prepared it: lamb cutlets from the local butcher, a salad, and red wine with a curious, dusty taste. Afterwards I cleared the table and went into the kitchen to wash up. Through the window I watched some clouds in the sky, charred black within, running molten at their edges; then they suddenly turned pink – an absurd, childish colour, which seemed to have nothing to do with the fierce calcinations of a moment before. Later green and indigo lights appeared. I had almost finished the job when I heard Ritchie's voice rise high, like a hysterical boy's. "Then I'm leaving," he yelled. "Who needs him here? Who asked him to come? Shit!" These words were followed by a thump. He must have banged his fist on a table or kicked away a chair. I heard Dafne enter the house and go upstairs to her bedroom. Ritchie came into the kitchen through the door that opened on the back garden, and stood blinking in the electric light, a dark green space of sky behind him. Veering and wobbling at the end of his neck, his face looked patchy, smaller than ever.

"One day I'm going to kill the bastard," he announced.

"Who?"

"Max," he enunciated with a would-be feminine toss of his head, as if imitating his mother.

"Who?"

"Max," he repeated. "Spass. The fucking First Treasurer."

164

He minced excruciatingly again. "Her lover-boy."

"You?" I said. "Kill him? Don't make me laugh."

More veering and wobbling. But he kept his brown eyes fixed on mine.

"You think I couldn't do it?"

"I know you couldn't."

His voice broke. "I thought you believed in me," he said childishly.

I wiped the sink. The veined, yellowing porcelain looked like the skin of an old woman. The dishes were stacked in a gleaming row. I wrung out the cloth and hung it up.

"Well," I answered in quite a different tone, "I would like to."

A moderate reply. A deliberate reply. One that he had provoked me to make.

I didn't expect him to return to the subject the next day. And the day after that. The more he raved, the more scornfully I found myself responding. His face went pale at my words; his eyes darkened from within. It was a look that filled me with lust: with a lust to see that same look yet again. He obliged me. He always came back for more.

He brought me the stories he had written while he had been alone in the cottage. His handwriting was earnest and childish; so were the stories. Full of filthy words, dream sex, faecal images, and much detailed violence, most of them featured a villain – variously named Piss, S., M., the Big Shot – who was continually being impaled, burned, torn in two by cars pulling in opposite directions, driven mad by "Control" at "Thought Centre 6" through the radio receivers planted in his head, crucified on electric pylons, and so forth.

Then he asked me what I had made of them.

That time, too, my reply was very restrained. I tossed back to him, with a single comment, the exercise book which contained the stories.

"Words are cheap."

On another occasion he said that Spass was just like a snake: all gleamy and slimy and twisty. Even his name was a snake-name. And what did people do with snakes? They killed them. They put a pitchfork through the back of their scaly necks, didn't they?

I said wearily, "There you go again." And later, "What does it feel like to know that you're all talk – talk, talk, talk?" Whereupon, irritated by the sight of his protruding lower lip (it embarrasses me to confess this), I took hold of my own lip between thumb and forefinger, and waggled it up and down, sticking my face as close to his as I could.

Such childishness. Such triviality. I won't give any further examples of our colloquies on the subject. What's the point? Yet I insist that it would be wrong to conclude that I had a precise, coldly calculated end in view throughout. Not at all! I wouldn't have been clever enough. In any case I was too besotted by him. Listening to his tirades, jeering at him for indulging in them, mocking him and challenging him, I could hardly breathe at the pressure of anger and affection within me. Calling him a fool, a weakling, a spoiled child, a talker, a wanker, I wanted to strangle and caress him; to take into my own lungs all the "smoke" or vagueness that was inside his swaying head; to leave in its place hardness, determination, ruthlessness. But how remote that trans-formation still seemed! Then I would be able to love and pity him wholeheartedly. Forever. Or so I thought, in my infatuation.

Thus, coil upon coil, negation upon affirmation, and affirmation upon denial, until the terms lose their meaning, we tighten the springs within us that any tilt, any jolt, any shock, can suddenly release.

The night before Spass was expected, I came upon Ritchie keeping vigil on a little terrace beneath the window of his mother's room. It was some time after midnight. I have no idea how long he had been there. Not a foot away from me he stood quite still, hopelessly still, as if trying to convince me that he wasn't there, or at least that I should kindly consider him to be invisible. His face was nothing more than some tips of skin, and a glitter that came and went where his eyes should have been. The evening was absolutely calm. There was no moon. No sound came from the bedroom above. I put a hand between his shoulder-blades and pushed him gently forward: with such contemptuous gentleness, such lethal kindness, I was positively afraid I would reel backwards from the sheer pressure of it within my arm. Before he floated away from my touch, I felt the warmth of his skin on my fingertips, through the thin shirt he was wearing. In the starlight I saw a fixed smirk of shame beneath his moustache. He did not allude to the incident the next morning. Only his eyes spoke of it. No doubt mine answered.

A moment ago I wrote of the jolt or shock that can unleash a coiled spring within us, impelling us into action. Paradoxical though it may seem, I believe that that scarcely palpable, instantly retracted touch of my hand on Ritchie's back may have done the trick. But not directly. Not at once. Not in the way anyone could have anticipated.

The next day Spass arrived, as arranged. He did not stay in the cottage, but in a rather grander house he had rented up in the foot-hills. Despite the passage of time, despite his promotions, despite the unsavoury rumours one heard about the manner in which he had gained those promotions, including his part in the suppression of the last Kuni uprising, he had changed little since I had known him from my days in the Ministry of National Guidance. He was still so watchful, so restrained, so inexpressive, he was somehow more like an impersonation of a man than a real human being. Even his looks seemed to be less the result of chance and heredity than of conscious choice. His trim figure and smooth skin; his nervous hands and charged, sibilant manner of speaking; the oiled, chestnut, youthful waves of his hair, which I suspected him of dyeing; his immaculate clothes; the distant blue gleam of his eyes – all might have been specially acquired for an ulterior purpose it was better not to guess at. He was always formal and correct with Dafne, while she was more brusque then ever when he was around; shyer, stiffer, more uneasy. I have no notion what they were like à deux. I can't even begin to imagine it. Whenever I try, all I see are scenes from her old movies.

Such a man would never have been my chosen companion for a scramble up the Enckelberg. Nor Ritchie's, obviously. Yet less than a week after his arrival we were on the mountainside with him, together with Jordaan, his bodyguard. Why? Because Spass himself had suggested it. If he didn't do the climb soon, he'd said, he would never do it; he was getting so old. Dafne had seconded the idea. (Not that she intended accompanying us.) Inevitably, we had accepted the challenge.

So there we were, surrounded by immensities of light and space: hillsides overhead bigger than the sky; valleys below withholding the secrets of their last recesses; the Great Lecke Lake slowly coming into view, bit by bit, beyond the furthest mauve mass on what had hitherto been the horizon; each slope we toiled across seeming to promise us a final rest if only we could surmount it, and then revealing the one above and behind it, in endless fold upon fold. But I also remember from our first day's march the pattern on a single veined stone momentarily lying in my path. The bare, worn, whitish, naked heel of Moses, our guide, with the skin over his tendon wrinkled horizontally, and supple, like the trunk of an elephant. A fragment of eggshell and a dried filament of yolk caught on a blade of grass. And the colours of barrenness and growth, nearness and distance, in an ever-recurring range, while clouds and sky exchanged blues and whites and sunset reds, and joined together at nightfall in a common black: all of them faintly hazed, even the black, as if the air, too, had a colour of its own, which one could never name, but which took something from all the others.

Strange, in spite of everything, how joyous and free so many of my memories of that outing remain. Even Moses I remember with affection, though I don't suppose we exchanged more than a dozen sentences, either before or after the catastrophe. He was a secretive, half-caste Kuni, with disproportionately long legs in khaki trousers, who went barefoot for the first part of the journey. It was not until the following morning that he took a pair of ancient, laceless boots out of his bag and put them on. He whistled between his teeth as he strutted along; and, having seen how Spass had been treated by the authorities at the lodge, solemnly called him "My Lord".

We slept the night in a wooden hut on a heather-covered

plateau; one of a group of huts put there for the convenience of climbers. We had occasionally seen other parties during the day, and had been overtaken a couple of times, for we suited our pace to that of Spass, the oldest of us. He was obviously determined to finish the climb; he was also making sure that he would not over-tire himself in doing so. Our intention was to spend a second night on the mountain, in a hut just below the summit.

I slept too well to know how the others managed on their bunks. But I was the first to get up in the morning, except for Moses, who had spent the night in a little tent of his own. I found him making a fire outside. Its smoke rose with a curious haste straight into the air, as if it were determined to disappear as rapidly as possible into the spaces above. The sun had not yet risen; the heather smelled of the moisture it had gathered during the night; lazy white fish-shapes of mist, seeming to feed upon the headlands to which they were moored, filled the valleys below. The damp, grey, still world had the aspect of eternity upon it – revealed once again, ready for that morning as for how many millions before. Above us hung the bluff we would have to circumnavigate later that morning. Rock-face foremost, like a shield, with a single crooked tree on a shelf half-way up, it waited patiently for the sunlight to strike it.

We breakfasted, washed, went off with bits of paper into hollows in the ground and returned a little later without them. The sun came up; the mist turned pearl and gold, making it even more opaque than before, and suddenly vanished.

Soon after setting out we left the heather that had been under-foot for much of the previous day and entered a region of rock, gravel, sand, slippage, and, high up, in patches and streaks sheltered from the sun, like white shadows, the traces of the winter's snow. Though the bluff had seemed so close above us, we did not round it until midday. Then we saw what lay ahead: the great basin or amphitheatre, hitherto concealed, in which we would be marching the rest of the day. There was no sunshine within it; no water; its colours were light grey scratched with darkness, dark grey scratched with white, an unreflecting blue.

Our path ran along an unbroken ledge well below its rim. To the left the mountainside rose sheer; on the right there was a drop almost as precipitous of about a hundred metres. That so huge a place should have been so enclosed, like the interior of a crater, made it seem all the more desolate at first sight; even uncanny. A wind blew inside it: never constant, never ceasing.

There was no danger in all this, however. The ledge was a couple of metres wide and had been carefully maintained. In several places erosion-gulleys had been filled in, and little dry-stone parapets had been built up for hundreds of metres at a stretch where the path narrowed. Only if a mist or storm came down suddenly would there be any risk; and neither of these was expected. Besides, Moses was supposed to know what to do under those conditions, too; the guides, as we had been told at the lodge, in the inevitable phrase, knew their way around the mountain blindfold.

Well, we marched forward on our pathway, balanced between a vertical solidity on one side and empty space on the other. The curve within the amphitheatre turned out to be by no means as smooth as it had appeared from a distance; the cliff-face was riven with crevices and rock-falls, some of them massive, and our path had to follow every irregularity and corrugation in it. Thus we often found ourselves out of sight of one another; sometimes the two members of the party closest together would be unable to see each other, while someone much farther behind or ahead would be visible to them both.

We had talked little the previous day; now we talked not at all. Yet our progress was noisier than before, because of the blurred sound of the wind within our ears, and the sharp clicking of stones underfoot. Moses kept up his whistling, a small, dying sibilance, like that of a kettle taken off the boil; when you expected it to lapse into silence it would start up again.

Every time I looked up it seemed I had just missed seeing the vast, silent cliff reel into the place above me it now occupied. So I kept my head down.

The hours passed. Slowly we strung ourselves out. Jordaan

was at the head, with Moses following him; Spass and Ritchie brought up the rear; I was in the middle. Towards midday I had got so far ahead of the stragglers I decided to wait for them. The parapet had been built up at that point, and I sat down gingerly on it, facing inwards. The skin of my back crawled a little, as if a current of some kind were pulling at it from the abyss below. But I would rather have had the emptiness at my back than that ever-toppling, ever-motionless cliffside.

I heard Ritchie before I saw him. Feet or hands scrambled, stones flew. Then he appeared around a large, buttress-like outcrop of rock. His gait was so disjointed, the look on his face so distraught, I jumped up with one word in my mind – "Accident!" (Only later did it occur to me that that alone showed how little faith I had in him!) He rushed and faltered forward, arms out as if to embrace me, and collapsed on the ground next to the wall, practically at my feet. He was trembling violently. He tried to speak – once, a second time. From the back of his throat he finally managed to produce some words.

"I can't do it! It just needed a push –! He was sitting there – I couldn't –"

Spass came round the flank of the mountainside. Ritchie covered his face with both hands.

It seemed to take a long time for Spass to draw near. From his expression it was obvious he knew something had happened between them. It was clear too that he did not really know what it was; or what it had meant. He looked more puzzled than angry or frightened. He halted a few paces away and stared curiously at Ritchie.

There was no sound, other than that of the wind, like a wavering film or obstruction right inside the ear, which one could never get rid of. I was the first to speak: laboriously, without excitement, as if carrying out an inescapable, wearisome obligation.

"You see, sir," I explained, pointing at Ritchie, "he wants to push you over the side. But he can't do it. He hasn't got the nerve. He just told me so."

Spass's face changed.

"What?"

The word had risen automatically to his lips; it wasn't a question, just an exclamation.

So I repeated what I had said.

Again – without movement, somehow – his expression altered. Again he exclaimed: "What?"

"Ask him," I said.

Ritchie still sprawled alongside the little wall, his hands covering his face. I bent over him and shouted, "Isn't that right, Ritchie? Didn't you say so? You tried but you couldn't do it, hey! You've been dreaming about it ever since we got on the mountain, haven't you? Haven't you, damn it?"

"Yes," Ritchie cried from behind his hands, and huddled closer to the wall.

"There you are," I said to Spass. "I thought you should know."

He had come forward a pace or two.

"I think I should."

I touched Ritchie with my foot. Just a touch.

"Come on, you can get up now."

He hurled himself at me, from where he lay on the ground. I saw his eyes. I heard the snarl in his throat. I felt his hands tear at my collar. Then I had him pinioned with both arms behind his back. He was struggling, twisting, trying to turn towards me. We were no more than half a metre from the parapet. I glanced at Spass. His face was truly like a snake's – narrow lips drawn back, eyes shining.

He nodded, distinctly, unmistakably, as if giving me an order. I feinted, pushing Ritchie forward and jerking him back. I looked at Spass again. He came closer.

"Yes," he whispered, staring at me, not Ritchie. "I say yes."

My honour was at stake. You know! Was I a serious person or not? Was I Ritchie Mainckies – or Josef Baisz? Which?

A rescue team brought Ritchie's body down to the wardens' lodge the following day. I do not know which was worse: the change that had come over his face, or the change that had not. It was destroyed. It had ceased to be. Yet I had seen before the expression of terror and disbelief that was still fixed upon it.

XXI

DESCRIBING THE VIEW over Port Margriet from the balcony of my flat, I omitted to mention the waterfront and the straggle of cranes and masts alongside it. Tucked away among these was a small coastguard station, where a launch was kept for the use of the authorities on Volmaran Island. At 9 a.m. exactly, on most weekday mornings, I would board that launch, together with others among my colleagues who lived in the city, and we would set out on our journey towards the island: a low, uneven, blue-grey protuberance above the water, with a few spires or spikes sticking out from it.

I made the crossing in all conditions: with the lake glittering under the lavishments of the sun; with thunder-clouds racing each other overhead, like flocks or herds whipped to a frenzy by the wind; in blind, seasonless times of mist, when black and silver light dripped off the flanks of every sluggish wavelet set in motion by the launch itself. But never did I know the magic of landfall to fail, even after such a short journey. The island swung up like another world, each time; stepping out upon it always felt like another birth.

From the quay a paved road ran through the officers' quarters – small, whitewashed houses of regulation government design – to the first perimeter gate and fence. Then the second. Then the third. At last one had entered the prison compound proper. Huts, wire, guardrooms, big corrugated iron workshops in which motors howled incessantly, loud-speakers on poles, an infirmary – the whole place was spread out over a much greater area than one would ever have guessed, seeing it from the water. There were acres of vegetable garden, and stretches of trodden flint and mud between each group of huts. Double lines of fences, with space between them for a patrolling man and dog, ran maze-like in all directions, and met here and there in knots or clusters; from each of these clusters rose a guard-tower, surmounted by a conical roof. In the very middle of the camp was the old monastery, a handsome group of stone buildings extensively rebuilt from within, which housed the prison headquarters.

My office was on the top floor, at the end of a spiral staircase. At about 9.40 a.m. Josef Baisz, bodyguard to hundreds, took his seat behind his desk, and began the day's work.

Bodyguard? Soulguard rather. Spiritguard. Mindguard.

At last, after so many false starts it seemed that I had found my true métier. I had become guide and spiritual counsellor to those much less fortunate than myself.

In other words, I had initiated and then been appointed to the post of Moral Guidance Officer to Volmaran Corrective Labour Colony. One part of my job was to convince the press, the public at large, the Prison Commissioners, church bodies, visiting delegations from abroad, and all other interested parties, that the "socially injurious elements" incarcerated in the Volmaran camp truly regretted all the wrong they had done in the past, and were now loyal citizens of the Republic, eager to contribute whatever they could to its well-being and power. The most efficient way of achieving that end was to persuade sufficient numbers of prisoners that that was how they actually felt. An important and taxing assignment, you will agree; one in which my special talents could be fully used.

I had been a great success in the job right from the start. None of the education officers and chaplains who had been employed in the penal system for decades had ever produced results like mine. It was my prisoners who produced the tapestry depicting the Centraad rising to applaud the Heerser, which now hangs in the foyer of the new party headquarters. It was my prisoners who spontaneously petitioned the Ministry of Justice to extend their sentences by periods of up to three years, in order to demonstrate the sincerity of their remorse over their past wrongdoings. My prisoners who voluntarily proposed a cut of thirty percent in their bread rations, after the great crop failure of two years ago. My prisoners who urged the Heerser to bestow upon the governor of the island the Faal Ribbon of Merit, in recognition of his services on their behalf. They could be sent anywhere, my prisoners, with perfect confidence in what they would say and do, before any audience: any commission of inquiry, or international tribunal, or newspaper or radio interviewer. When Stanford Peech, the famous American investigator, declared that in all his experience of visiting penal institutions he had never come across a group of men so eager to repay the state for all it had done for them, he was speaking of my prisoners. And when the great French philosopher, M. J-J. Delport, wrote of seeing with his own eyes that men under pressure could indeed "reconstruct their souls", as he put it, he was speaking of the souls I had reconstructed.

I could go on in this vein: but I won't, lest I be accused of boasting.

The secret of my success? By now it should be no secret at all. When the prisoners came into my office (or into the "Moral Guidance Centre" which I had set up further down the main road through the camp, beyond the punishment block) they felt at once how different my attitude was from any they were likely to meet elsewhere. Outside my office was a place of mud, wooden huts, electric lights burning night and day; noise, cold, insufficient food; armed guards, parades, exhausting labour; countings, niggardly privileges, profuse punishments, and an unrelenting gregariousness; the sight of ever-changing, unattainable land in the distance, and of the imprisoning water between, where coasters moved back and forth, and little sailing boats, their sails like leaves upended, turned and bellied out as they caught the wind, under a sky in which clouds assembled and dispersed for no reason, day after day. And no end to any of it.

But here, in a quiet, curtained, carpeted room, was their Moral Guidance Officer: eager to listen, to understand, to reassure, to make large promises. True, he was a servant of the regime that was inflicting upon them the diurnal misery they were undergoing. But that made all the more irresistible the goodwill that he alone showed to them! How difficult it was for them *not* to believe that he had their welfare at heart when he squeezed their arms, gazed into their eyes, smiled and bent his head to catch their whispers. Who could speak more intimately to them of the sufferings they had undergone even before their imprisonment, of the sufferings that had indeed led to their imprisonment – the injustices they had seen, the humiliations they had endured, the lies they had been expected to swallow; or of the rebellious impulses that had seized them, and that had grown more plausible, and hence more frightening, every time they had recurred, until in the end it may have been to escape or silence their own fears that they had plunged into the very action that had so frightened them? Who knew more than Josef Baisz about the shame they felt as they listened to him; the nauseating thrill of the thought of succumbing to his blandishments; the astounding sense of absolution and liberation, of being beyond any possible forgiveness, and therefore of no longer needing it, which was the ultimate reward for every act of betrayal and self-betrayal? Who could take more pleasure than Josef Baisz when the rewards he promised for their cooperation were delivered: parole, or transfer, or visits from wives or children, or extra letters or parcels?

Admittedly, the prisoners who were given to me were of a special kind. I didn't deal with ordinary thieves and rapists and murderers – though there were plenty of these in the camp, as of every sort of offender. I worked only with those who had committed crimes against the state. One could say that my special brief was to take care of the political prisoners. (Except that no such category of persons exists in terms of our law.) My prisoners were by no means all dissident ideologues, however, or members of underground organisations, or rebellious workmen, or disgraced politicians, or Kuni and Sedi nationalists. So much of our trade, industry, and agriculture are in the hands of the state that many people came to me who in another country might have been thought of merely as crooks or fools. All of them, moreover, had been sentenced to long terms (five years and upwards), of which they had served at least half. Thus they were worn out by what had passed, and even more disheartened by the thought of what was to come.

When I think of the prisoners now I can clearly see individual faces and recall individual names. They appear in endless parade before me, opening their mouths, repeating the phrases I dropped into them, tasting with every shade of repulsion and appetite the poisoned bait I proffer them. Not a movement of a muscle of their faces, not a flicker of their eyes, not a turn of the head, but tells me its story, reveals to me what I no longer want to know but am condemned (for a little longer) to remember. But when I try to recall my audience – delegations, journalists, visitors, and so forth – no individuals appear: all I see is a pair of earnest spectacles, worn indiscriminately by male and female, and a shared look of uplift and apprehension. There was no art in hoodwinking them. They wanted to be hoodwinked. If they hadn't wished to be deceived they would never have been permitted to come. No wonder they so readily murmur their appreciation of the wonderful, patient work of regeneration we are doing; smile in stern but kindly fashion at the renegades we are all so anxious to reform; step back thankfully into the launch that will carry them back to the mainland.

So. I trust that I haven't made my appointment sound too glamorous. Basically it was just a job, like any other. In fact, I was surprised at first to find out how much, even for the prisoners themselves, the colony itself functioned for the most part like any other organisation or institution that simply had to be kept going. There were routines to be followed; office politics and rivalries to engage in; accounts to be balanced; bribes to be accepted or refused; indents for supplies to be filled in; campaigns to be conducted over space and facilities; bad days when the prisoners were mutinous or when punishment parades were held; good days when letters or parcels were distributed, or the staff had their parties and the prison-band and the prison-singers were brought in to entertain them. The chief difference between this work-place and every other was that ours had just one impalpable product, for which it used one irrecoverable raw material. The product was misery; the raw material, time.

The workshops turned out coat-hangers, stamped metal ash-trays, and wooden furniture; but these items were merely incidental to the main purpose of the entire establishment. Its operations, I should add, were highly departmentalised. Nobody asked me what I did with my prisoners in the hours when I had them to myself. I did not ask the people in the punishment block what they did with theirs. Sometimes, though, the prisoners would tell me; and I would grieve with them over what they had suffered.

At the end of each day the launch carried me back to the mainland. Another landfall. A more grandiose one this time: to an open, bustling city, with cars and trams and flickering electric signs. I would go up the hill to my home and its pleasures. And its prisoners.

They were always glad to see me. Having greeted them affectionately, and poured myself a drink, I would usually step on to the balcony and look out over the city and across the lake, and try to make out the contours of the island. Only very rarely would it be possible. Overhead the sky would be rose, red, grey, filled with light and colour, without surface. Beneath me distances were abolished and protracted in ways which I could never understand: streets intersected one another at odd angles; trees along pavements showed themselves at unexpected places; lit-up shop-windows gleamed in gaps between buildings. Small figures continually passed below; in apartments across the street I saw people coming and going in rooms I would never enter. The noise of cars, of curtains being drawn, of music, cries, and voices speaking faintly, all ascended in a hiss and murmur to the sky. Then I would be called in for dinner.

So things could have gone on, perhaps for years. I had nothing to fear. The job would always have been mine. There was no likelihood of my post ever being abolished. If I had been content to remain a valued but relatively unnoticed servant of the state, I could still be there. You could say that I have been punished for over-reaching myself. Perhaps. Yet that which actually brought about my ruin was nothing. Such a little matter, compared to what I already had on my conscience. A trifle.

XXII

TIME RUNS OUT, my story draws to an end, I have only a single day and night before the period I asked for is over. Yet I find myself beleaguered more insistently than ever by random memories from long ago. One part of my mind says that they are quite irrelevant to the events that brought me here; another asks – how can they be? There isn't a moment of my life, remembered or unremembered, which didn't help to bring me here. I lived through them all.

All ages are equal in the sight of God, some historian once said: an Englishman, I think. I may have got the quotation wrong or mistranslated it. Well, in the same way all moments in his life should be equal in value to a dying man.

Therefore I interrupt my description of life in Port Margriet to say that a minute ago, for no reason I am conscious of, I remembered how my father used to swing me in the air when I was a little boy. Like all fathers with their children, I suppose, he would stand behind me, put a hand in each of my armpits, and swing me back through his open legs and forward into the air, over and over again. As I went forward I would kick my feet up over my head, so that he had to lean back to avoid getting them in his face. While swinging me he sang the special nonsense song which was such an important part of the game. *Hinja, pinja, pila, poocks*: those were its words. Only when he was panting, and his face had gone quite patchy with the exertion, would he say, "No more, I'm exhausted. You're getting too heavy for me."

Finally I did get too heavy for him. The game came to an end.

Another memory, also suddenly emerging from nowhere: from a different time, anyway. All it has in common with the last is a certain rhythm. And legs. At the age of about fifteen I went on a picnic with my class, to a local beauty spot. (A river, a spit of sand, some trees.) In the evening, coming home on the back of an open lorry, I shared a blanket with a girl called Lena Miro. Under it, I put my hand between her legs. The warmth there was amazing; so were her powers of dissimulation. She chattered to me, and to the people on both sides of us, as if quite unconscious of the steady contractions and relaxations of her thighs around my hand. Until she suddenly caught her breath, crossed her legs, and was silent for fully two minutes.

End of digression. (If it was a digression: I simply don't know.) Back to Port Margriet. No, a little further back. Back to the very last visit I made to Boschoff. This was well before my posting to Port Margriet and my job on Volmaran Island; before my marriage to Trude; indeed, before I had met Trude again. I was a student, then, in my second semester at Ronaldsflai College. One morning, while I was in residence there, a telegram from Beata arrived. It announced baldly that our mother had died. Apparently she had collapsed in the street and was dead before any help could be brought to her.

So, like a dutiful son, and brother, I went straight up to Boschoff. I remember feeling as surprised, somehow, just to be back in the town as I was by the occasion that had brought me there. None of what I saw and did during that visit seemed quite real to me: not even when I followed the coffin to the grave, together with Beata, the children, and, of all people, Fenter's mother. She had grown much older and more flaccid since I had last seen her. Nobody else. Fenter himself had decamped several months before, with his lady-friend.

The cemetery was a sloping, littered piece of ground on the outskirts of the city. Discreetly covered by a black cloth, mounted on a squeaking, high-wheeled trolley, the coffin was pushed forward by several men I had never seen before. A pastor went ahead. The sun shone, but the day was misty, milky, uncertain of itself; gleaming patches of obscurity lay between distant groups of buildings, roads, playing-fields, water-towers. No sound came from them. We walked in procession along a gravelled pathway. The rounded tombstones on both sides of the path were like the heads of reclining people, lifted to see us go by. No one cried. At the graveside the pastor pointed his shaven chin at the horizon and spoke of my mother's immortal soul. Then the men set to work to fill the grave. High notes rang from little stones, in the midst of their gruff shovellings.

Afterwards we went back to the flat for a meal. Beata assured me that she was making ends meet by working behind a counter in a shop, and from what the Social Benefits people paid her. Her mother-in-law helped too, especially in looking after the children. I gave her money for the funeral expenses, and a little over.

And that was that. As soon as I could get away, I left for the station. With my mother gone there seemed to be nothing to keep me and Beata together. I would never, never have expected this beforehand; it would have seemed quite inconceivable to me; yet it was true. To think that she had had that power over us! Now it was gone. The discharge from the family which I had so often longed for had at last been given to me. I left with no intention of keeping in touch with Beata; nor did I do so.

I returned to Ronaldsflai to resume my studies. I was attending the college on a bursary which Spass, my new patron, had procured for me; my subjects were history and psychology; I had had the vague intention, in going to Ronaldsflai, of perhaps becoming a pastor in due course. The college was not a seminary, but there was one nearby to which it was attached; and most of the students proceeded there after graduation. On my return, however, I found that I could no longer sink myself into the company of the earnest, conventional young men, anxious to oblige their superiors and eventually to secure good positions for themselves in the state church, who were my companions there.

Nor could I take pleasure any longer in the college and its surroundings.

As before I attended my classes; I went for walks around the shallow, circular depression of the lake, or flai, which, like some great lidless eye staring forever upwards, vacantly reflected all it saw. But the excitement of making a fresh start, of acquiring a disguise which no one would ever be able to penetrate, had gone out of all I did. I could not sleep. As each day began its slow work of dawning I sat at the window of my cubicle, watching the sky turn watery and the lake harden like metal. The black mass on the far side gradually disclosed the shapes of the trees that made it up. Within the dormitory a lavatory would clank like a chained beast, before uttering its first roar of the day.

Even now I do not know whether my mother's death was the cause of the state I fell into. I cannot even describe it; or can do so only by saying that it was a foreshadowing of the condition that was to bring me here and compel me to write these words – though at the time no such expedient occurred to me. Nothing occurred to me. I was blank, null, empty, incapable of emotion, barely capable of speech. I had known spells of indolence before, spells of inactivity and melancholy; but never anything like this.

It ended, this period of psychic paralysis, with an outburst that also brought to an end my residence as a student at the institution. We had been having a seminar at the lakeside, where many of our classes were held; I can't remember now what the topic was. Afterwards I went for a walk with three fellow-students, nicknamed Frog, Melon and Sailor, respectively. (Everyone, without exception, had a nickname that year; mine was "Bril" – an obscure reference to the dark glasses I affected.) To my own surprise, as well as that of the others, I found myself launched upon a damagingly candid account of certain events in my childhood and adolescence I had never spoken of before to anyone. I didn't get really far into that chronicle, however, before I was distracted into a confused kind of allegory or parable based upon the life of Jesus. Judas, I told them, had been the exemplar and hero of my green youth. But what was he compared with the one who had filled Jesus' head with ideas of a divine provenance, who had encouraged him to believe in his miraculous powers, had urged him to challenge the authorities of the day . . . and then, when he met the punishment meted out for such presumption, and cried out in agony from the cross, had quietly and expertly absented himself from the scene? That was the real point of the story, which had gone too little noticed for all these years –

I abbreviate the speech I made; I have to, since I went on at such length. My companions, all of them destined for careers in the church, listened to me with alarm and fascination. With every word I spoke I was rediscovering the pleasure, known only to truly deceitful people, of confession. The pleasure also of the degradation it inflicts on those compelled to listen. (Or read . . .) A series of frowns moved across the broad, vacant brow of old Frog, the slowest and heaviest of my auditors; next to him, already adjusting himself to the prospect of a scandal, stood Melon, a lithe, sly, self-satisfied creature, with a pumpkin-shaped head that gave him a wholly specious air of candour. And then there was Sailor, who had been my companion several times on expeditions to the neighbouring town of Faures, where we had visited a few bars, or the one, oddly suburban brothel of which the place boasted. (Complete, it was, with a wide verandah, cannas in the garden, and a bicycle invariably parked in an alleyway to the side.)

Sailor was the first to speak. I could see what an effort it was for him to do so. "Josef –" he said warningly. But I waved away his interruption. So he hit me on the temple, quite hard, with his clenched fist. Strange how the whole world can suddenly compact itself to a single object, a hard thing, a lump of blackness. I came to on the grass. Only a moment had passed. Frog was looking anxiously at me.

That was all. I got to my feet and we went on with our walk. It was in this dazed, dislocated fashion, however, with the domes and columns of the college to one side of me – and in front of me too, reflected in the wavering water of the lake, as if I were seeing double, from the blow I had just received – that I first discerned the outlines of a new kind of career. The idea was a simple one really, though revolutionary for me. Enough concealment! Time to go public!

From that point on I began to recover. Melon did his bit to help. He reported our conversation to the gentleman with the imposing title of Ordinarius, who was in charge of the students' moral discipline. He in turn challenged me with my words. I admitted to all of them, and refused to retract any. I was already on my way out. On my way back to Bailaburg.

Spass was my only hope of promotion there. But I did not look him up, after returning to the capital, until I had further restored my morale by making contact with two earlier acquaintances: Trude Haifert and Gita Serle. Of Gita, more in a moment. The results as far as Trude was concerned you already know. What I haven't yet said is that it was my experience with her which put into my head the scheme for the "spiritual renovation" and "moral regeneration" of prisoners which I eventually placed before Spass.

Many unflattering things can be said about our system of government: it is clearly wasteful, cumbersome, bound about with every conceivable bureaucratic rigidity, etc. (I don't even speak of its morals here.) But it is also capable of moving at great speed when the right people apply pressure to it in the right places. So it was in this case. Without Spass I would have been nowhere. With him everything became possible. The scheme so captured his imagination that he put great effort into making sure that I remained attached throughout to my old department, the Ministry of National Guidance, which still happened to be one of his fiefdoms, and did not transfer to the Ministry of Justice, which was nominally in charge of the entire penal system.

I never became part of Spass's immediate entourage, however. The reason, of course, was his continuing relationship with Dafne. He even kept from her the fact that he was supporting me, and that we used occasionally to meet. Not that she blamed me for what had happened to her son. Not at all. She accepted the story we had told. Ritchie had been playing the fool. He had been walking along the edge of the parapet, showing off, indulging in a bit of bravado, when he had lost his balance and fallen. I had begged him to desist. To no avail. (You know what he was like.) Avoidable, yet fatally in character. Tragic, but stupid. That was the verdict.

XXIII

THINGS HAD NOT BEEN GOING WELL, I had found, with Gita and Serle. Serle's religious faith had not kept him from taking to drink; or from becoming slack, bald, stertorous, and incommunicative as a result. Gita was just weary. She was also depressed because she hadn't been able to conceive a child, which was something she had set her heart on. Doubly depressed about it, indeed: she was convinced her infertility was a judgment of some kind on the course of her whole life. Naturally I was involved in that judgment. Because she knew facts about me that were unknown to everyone else she now looked on me with a kind of horror. Still, she would not let me go.

We used to meet as before; sometimes in Serle's presence, sometimes alone. Of those meetings I will describe only the very last, which took place in a room in the Central Temperance Hotel – an institution as forbidding as its name. She had given Serle some excuse for her absence that night; a pretty perfunctory one, as I recall. I don't think he cared all that much about it, anyway. We went to bed early; then lay there in silence, side by side. Beams from the headlamps of cars passed across the ceiling: some in a great hurry, some tentative, all contracting to a sliver before they disappeared. Locomotives thudded in the distance. I fell asleep to the rhythm of Gita's breathing. Her heat woke me, much later, and I pulled her to me. "Go on! Go on!" she whispered abjectly; then cried and told me how much she still loved me. For that! I could hardly credit it. But I felt tender towards her, too. We lay tangled together, while areas of darkness in the room slowly became more and more solid, transforming themselves into objects: wardrobe, armchair, table. Elsewhere shadows thinned and withdrew, revealing the empty space they had occupied. Morning. Time to go.

Gita was the first up. She was just about ready to leave when I announced to her that Trude and I were going to get married shortly. She began to shiver and laugh. Her fingers couldn't manage the big green, cloth-covered buttons that ran all the way down the front of her dress.

"So you did kill him," she said, bowed over the task. "I knew it. I was always afraid of it."

"Nonsense," I answered, from the bed. "He shot himself. I was a hundred kilometres away when it happened."

"You must have killed him," she said, gulping and fumbling with the buttons. "Otherwise you wouldn't be marrying her. I know you. I know you too well."

She looked up, her face also fumbling, as it were, for an expression; then she gathered a few things into her bag and left the room.

That was the last time I saw her. Or ever shall see her.

But she will recognise the truth of all I've written here.

That wasn't the end of my dealings with the Serle–'S Koudenhoof family, however. Far from it. A good while after Trude and I were married and settled in Port Margriet, I wrote Gita a letter, telling her of our marriage, and also describing my new job – which I made out to be far more concerned with the social and spiritual welfare of the prisoners than it was. I didn't really expect a reply to this letter, and none came. But who should turn up in Port Margriet, as a result of it, if not her ne'er-do-well brother, Connie? In characteristically shifty and jaunty manner, he was looking for a job. I couldn't resist the temptation to help him. For the sake of his sister's brows and eyes, and certain of her quite unconscious movements of the head, all of which were his too, I had to do it. Especially after the admission, which he made with just the mixture of furtiveness and bravado one would expect, that he had known the truth about me and Gita "for years".

"From Gita?"

No, not from Gita.

"From who, then?"

He waited for a long time before giving his answer, evidently enjoying his own silence.

"From Kerrick."

"Kerrick!"

"Yes, I used to do bits of work for him. From time to time."

"You mean, when I first met you? When you were supposed to be involved with – what's its name – the Silver Fern?"

"I *was* involved with them," he said sulkily, almost indignantly.

I had to laugh. "And with Kerrick?"

He nodded. The look of peevishness on his face cleared, gave way to one of self-satisfaction. "I'm also an escapee, you know."

He was obviously referring to the collapse of the Compresecor. Another link between us! "Did Gita send you here?" I asked.

"Christ, no! It's just that I heard from her you had this job, and I wondered if there was anything I could do for you. Whether you might be able to fit me in somewhere. But I didn't tell her that I was coming. She'd have gone crazy if I had."

It didn't seem to worry him in the least that he was asking a favour of someone he had always despised and repeatedly tried to humiliate. I admired him for that, too.

Thus I acquired an assistant. At first he worked only on an *ad hoc* basis, mostly on "outside" work – helping arrange for publicity for my feats of persuasion and blackmail, thinking of new forms for these to take, organising the hospitality for the people who came to witness the results. Later he became a recognised part-time member of my tiny establishment, along with a few prisoners whom I used for clerical and secretarial work. Later still I managed to get him a formal appointment. He succeeded in making himself quite indispensable to me. After I had been attacked by an enraged prisoner just outside my office, Connie appointed himself my bodyguard, in addition to his other duties. It was a gesture (or jest) whose irony we both appreciated. He always came with me whenever I visited the island, or went on business to Bailaburg. He even insisted on accompanying me on this brief spell of leave, which I am ostensibly enjoying before taking up this new, exalted post to which the Heerser has appointed me.

He is outside now, somewhere in the village, as I write this.

I don't really know how he has been spending his time while I hammer away at these pages. We meet for meals, or to go for a walk in the evening, but talk little to one another. I have not told him what I've been doing, and I am careful to lock the door and window behind me every time I leave the room. I don't want to be distracted from my job by his questions or expostulations. Nor do I wish to put temptation of any kind in his way.

XXIV

NEARLY OVER. All that is left for me to do is to describe the last, great occasion of state I attended less than a fortnight ago, when our beloved Heerser announced through ringing loudspeakers, in the presence of hushed and attentive thousands, that I was to be promoted to the post of Deputy-Minister in the Ministry of National Guidance.

A moment of triumph. The reward for the work I had been doing. A prelude to much greater triumphs ahead. Who could deny it?

Only . . . before the Heerser made his announcement there took place this incident I have already referred to: this trifle, as I called it, which I am also obliged to describe.

Perhaps I and only one other person who was there that day even remember it now, though it happened so short a time ago. That's how insignificant it was. Yet its apparent insignificance to everyone else makes it all the more abominable to me. Decisive. Impossible to surmount or circumvent. Final, in fact.

The entire occasion, you see, was my doing. I had initiated it and organised it. It was my boldest propaganda stroke yet: a theatrical coup which in itself and by itself, I do believe, justified the promotion conferred on me. Nothing, not even the misfortune it brought upon me, will make me change that opinion.

Yet like most other startling ideas, this one was in essence simple enough. I had known for a long time that the Heerser, a man of fluctuating enthusiasms, had become increasingly interested in what could be called "penal reform". I had known also that my successes on Volmaran Island had been noted with approval by him; I had heard this both from Spass and from people within the Heerser's Bureau. Accordingly, I took it on myself to propose that the Heerser should pay a visit to the island on the occasion of some great national celebration.

At one moment such an idea would have seemed to me wild, absurd, even monstrous; the next, it had become obvious, self-evident, inevitable. But it still took my breath away.

(I was to have a somewhat similar experience a little later, when I decided to take myself to the mountains and write these memoirs.)

My intention was not for him to visit the island in order to triumph over his fallen enemies. Not at all! He would come to show his concern for even the least worthy of his people; his readiness to forgive those who were truly contrite; his compassion for those who had put themselves beyond everything but the reach of his power. So far from letting his enemies rot unseen in jail, as other rulers did; so far from being ashamed of the manner in which justice was administered on his behalf, as other rulers were, he would demonstrate to all his serene confidence in the humanity of his country's institutions and the love he bore for all his people. Our duty would be to see to it that this noble action received the widest possible publicity at home and abroad. Its effect, I was sure, especially if accompanied by an amnesty of some kind, would be sensational. It would be like the harrowing of hell by Jesus.

That was the scheme. I had to overcome a great deal of opposition, of course, before I could even get it presented to the Heerser; but I won't go into that story; it is too boring. Nor will I expatiate on the fact that those who had opposed my initiative most strenuously were the first to claim retrospective credit for having originated the idea, once the Heerser had shown an interest in it. I had quite as much of a struggle to make sure I wasn't elbowed out of my full share of recognition, at that stage, as I had had earlier to get the plan put before him. But I was successful in that effort too.

So it came about that barely two weeks ago, on Raitz Day, the celebration of one of our greatest military victories, I stood next to a specially erected platform to one side of the parade-ground in the centre of the camp. Thousands of others were waiting with me. Assembled since dawn, the prisoners stood in great oblong, close-packed blocks of drab grey, with a line of green-uniformed guards around each block. Even the women prisoners who lived on the far side of the camp, and were normally never allowed to mingle with the men, had been marched across from their quarters, and now stood in a block of their own, in front of the others. Everything in sight had been cleaned, swept, painted; even the stones that marked out the pathways through the camp had been freshly whitewashed. The camp-orchestra stood to one side of the platform ready to strike up the national anthem the moment the Heerser appeared. The guards, strengthened by a couple of battalions from the mainland, had never looked so "stick". Every button on their uniforms shone; light flowed like water over the surface of their boots; their collars rose stiff and identical to encase a variety of necks. Prisoners who fainted were carried away by special squads of their fellows, dressed in starched uniforms of a whiteness never before seen on the island. Talking was forbidden, of course. But every now and again the entire field of prisoners, like a great crop ready for harvesting, shivered and rustled from end to end.

The universal sense of expectancy, and the comings and goings of gloved and epauletted officers, reminded me vividly of my very first spell of service as Serle's bodyguard, when I used to attend great public occasions with him. But there were no tall buildings here; no street-corners; no cars; no meaningless outbursts of cheering and laughter; no children in school uniforms clutching little flags. Instead, stone and grey sky, low huts and straddled guard-towers with armed men upon them, silence and the smell of water. This was the place where power and powerlessness were to meet in naked confrontation, stripped of all disguise or palliation. Each was to know itself better, by looking face to face at its opposite. The truth about their relationship was to be made plain to all.

And who was responsible for this confrontation, this allegorical tableau? Who but Josef Baisz! To tell the truth, I was so proud of my achievement in bringing it about that I felt relatively indifferent, just at that moment, to the promotion which I knew to be coming my way.

A salute of cannon from the waterfront welcomed the Heerser to the island. Each thump was followed by a pause, a vacancy, a hollowness; one almost expected to see it, as well as feel it, as it passed through the air. But only the birds were sent whirling and clamouring into the sky. We waited. The birds drifted away, still complaining loudly. Minutes went by. We remained motionless. Then a sigh of longing and despair, like the wide hiss of a wave on a sandy beach, rose irrepressibly from a thousand throats.

There he was. The sound of the prisoners' welcome was instantly overtaken by a shout of command and the band striking up the national anthem. The Heerser stood to attention, in the midst of his party, hand lifted to the peak of his cap. On the last bar of the anthem he moved forward. I saw Spass behind him. His progress towards the dais was slow. All eyes followed it. The band was still playing. Now the prison-chorus had broken into "O Fatherland, My Country, You Are in Flames" – an anthem composed by Blick Mansfeld during Raitz's campaign.

Both band and chorus had fallen silent, however, by the time I was introduced to the Heerser. His gaze was waiting for mine, as I raised it. I saw blade upon tiny blade of light and colour in his eye, around a depthless pupil.

"Congratulations, Baisz."

"Your Excellency . . . !"

"Gouwerneur Spass has spoken well of you."

"Too kind . . . Your Excellency."

I was dizzied by the proximity of his stern, implausibly familiar face under the horizon of the peak of his cap. That the sounds emerging from his mouth were not grossly magnified surprised me faintly, like an act of kindness or condescension on his part.

"Your new duties will demand much of you, Baisz."

"Your Excellency –"

He resumed his advance towards the dais. I fell into place in the entourage, in accordance with the instructions issued to me long before. Spass's eye met mine; it acknowledged my existence and went elsewhere. We passed along the front row of the women prisoners, who were placed immediately before the dais. All this had been rehearsed many times, with soldiers and prisoners taking the place of the visitors.

Then it happened.

I know now that the incident was over in a minute or two. At the time I was conscious of intense flurries of noise and action, followed by what seemed like interminable passages of silence and immobility. I know what word was cried out from the ranks of the female prisoners. Then it sounded like nothing more than a mad, meaningless, shockingly indecorous yell.

Only the back of my neck and my spine knew better. They had recognised the voice which in front of thousands, before the Heerser himself, was yelling out my name.

XXV

I HEAR IT STILL.

"Jo-sef! Jo-sef! Jo-sef! Jo-sef!"

What followed wasn't even a period of waiting, for it seemed impossible that there should be an end to it. Yet there appeared to be a swaying, an eruption of some kind, taking place among the grey-overalled ranks nearest to us.

They struggled, they opened to eject something. A woman.

My sister, Beata.

I saw her face. Her eyes. Her shaven skull, as small as a monkey's. She was making straight for me. No one else moved, among all those thousands of spectators. In the same instant, it seemed, she was upon me; around me; clinging to me.

A dreadful stillness fell upon us both. I could not breathe or lift my hands. Time itself was paralysed. Then she was seized. I don't know by whom or by how many. The whole square, with all the people upon it, seemed to hang over us like a great wave. In the vacancy beneath, with Beata torn from me, suspended in the grasp of strangers, the Heerser turned. The tilt of his head gave his broad-jowled face a look of enquiry. But his eyes were quite expressionless.

"Do you know this woman?"

After another lapse, an absence of time, I shook my head.

He stared at me, offended by the gesture.

What I had done was not sufficient. I had to speak. To speak I had to shout.

"I know nothing about her!"

For the last time I saw Beata's eyes upon me. Her lips opened and closed over the syllables of my name. But she made no sound.

I hear that silence still.

XXVI

THAT WAS ALL. I mean, all that happened untowardly on the great day when the Heerser came to visit our island, and to reward me with such a substantial promotion for the efforts I had made. Everything else went off exactly as planned.

While the Heerser spoke I sat on the platform together with the other dignitaries, wearing on my face an expression of grave attention identical to theirs. Yet I heard little of what he said; and when my name was suddenly squawked out through the loudspeakers I felt no pride: only dismay, even horror, at being singled out again. Then my attention lapsed. Every time I looked at the female prisoners it seemed to me that their ranks had begun to heave and slither sickeningly, like water. Presently the Heerser announced the terms of his amnesty and the prisoners gave three cheers, as they had been authorised to do at that point. The sound was flat and echoless, in the great expanses that surrounded them.

Much later I went back on the launch to the mainland. I was surrounded by journalists busily getting drunk, now that the business of the day was concluded. Connie had seen to it that ample supplies of drink were available even on this little journey. He was talking and laughing among them. The trim little moustache he had grown was beaded with clear drops of slucke, which had always been his favourite tipple, even in the old days at the

Serles. Neither he nor any of the journalists asked me about the incident that had taken place earlier. Tact, as well as respect for my new position, inhibited them from doing so. Many of them, however, congratulated me on my promotion and assured me that they looked forward to working with me in the capital. "Great idea!" they said. "Wonderful!" But I could see in their drink-inflamed eyes how relieved they were to be out of the place we had just visited, and how they loathed me for having brought them there. Drunken, scribbling rubbish that they were, who would fill their columns with praise for our wonderful schemes of penal reform and the unheard-of magnanimity of the Heerser, they still looked at me as if I were tainted for belonging to the place.

I was. I was.

Yet I felt no remorse. I felt – nothing. It seemed to me I would never feel again. I wasn't even curious to know what Beata had done to bring her to the island. What difference did it make? She was there. She had called out my name. I had told the Heerser I knew nothing about her. She had seen me do it.

I left the journalists at the Press Club. Connie was still in charge. Ordinarily I would have stayed there for an hour or two. This time I went straight back to the apartment.

"How did it go, darling?" Trude asked.

"All right," I answered.

She was impeccably dressed, as always. Cream-coloured linen today. I saw in her eyes, and in the haggard lines of her face, a different but no more agreeable look than the one I had seen on the faces of the journalists. Hers was one of fear. There was nothing melodramatic about it. The expression was a habitual one. I had often noticed it before. I had always been rather proud of it. Today it roused no emotion; not pride, or contempt, or pity, or lust, or affection; none of what I had felt for her, in varying combinations, in the past. It was the same with the children. Their fear was lightened or brightened by sycophancy. So what? I could not understand why they, or their mother, were there, before me. She was another man's wife, or widow. They were another man's children. What did I have to do with any of them? I sat in my study and stared at the wall. Then I got up and went for a walk. I came home and went back into my study. Everyone was asleep. The hours passed.

I wanted to feel remorse. I would have welcomed it, for all its torments. It would have been a sign of life. It might even have presaged a readiness to forgive Beata for what I had done to her!

How could she bear to know what I was? How could I bear it that she knew?

Yet that wasn't remorse either.

The next day I was supposed to go to the island. I could not do it. I won't say that I was frightened to go. Rather, the idea filled me with an invincible repugnance. The knowledge that Beata was there made it insufferable to me. I did not want to see her again. I imagined her open mouth and shaven head, her skinny arms and staring eyes, waiting for me round every corner, at the end of every pathway, filling every barred window. I would find her sitting in my office. She would call out to me again. Everybody would come running.

Here was something new! People who had meant nothing to me I had betrayed and loved. But not Beata. Having denied and disowned Beata, who had been a cherishing and nourishing presence within my consciousness since its dawning, before its dawning, I felt only repugnance, even hatred, for her.

And the others? Now? As if through a breach she had made, that repugnance spread back, minute by minute, hour by hour, to engulf all the others, my beloved victims of the past. The inner estrangement I had felt from Trude and the children the previous night had merely been the first indication of what was about to take place within me. Ritchie, Gita, Serle, Haifert, lesser figures in my life, even Kerrick and Anton, all the prisoners I had got to perform such antics – individually and collectively the thought of them filled me with nothing but horror and revulsion. I loathed them. Loathed them for what I had done to them.

I was the carrier or vessel of this loathing; I gave it the only shape it had; it gave me the only function or purpose I had.

200

What a shape! What a purpose! How perfectly they matched my new appointment, which I had dreamed of for so long!

I did not go to the island. Instead, through pouring rain, I set out for the city library. On the way I bought a newspaper with "full story and pictures" of the Heerser's visit to the island. There was nothing in it about my promotion; but that didn't surprise me; such announcements were often not made until weeks or months after they had come into effect. In the library, under a distant dome of glass intersected by thin metal spokes and circles, like a spider's web, I went through the files of the *Boschoff Courant*. A sedate light fell upon barren plains of polished wood, and on vertical cliff-faces of brown and gilt leather bindings. Students around me went on with their work, amid a reverential rustle of paper. But I hung motionless over a single page: a full report of Beata's trial.

The case was simple enough. Fenter, it appeared, had embezzled money from his new employers in Baickondorff, where he and his lady-friend had gone to live. The shortfall had been discovered only after he had bolted. The police had then approached Beata and told her that she should inform them immediately if he were to turn up and ask for help – which he did, several weeks later. Beata had not handed him over to the police. Instead she had fed him, clothed him, and kept him hidden in the flat. Finally a neighbour had informed against them both. Fenter had managed to get away; Beata stood trial for having aided him.

Public Prosecutor : You knew this man was a fugitive. You had been told what to do if he came to you for help. Why did you disobey your instructions?

Accused : I felt sorry for him.

Public Prosecutor : Even though you knew he had committed a serious criminal offence?

Accused : Yes.

Public Prosecutor : What would happen if everyone behaved in the same way?

Accused : (Inaudible.)

Public Prosecutor : Louder, accused.

Accused : He is my husband.

Public Prosecutor : Your husband? He was living in Baickon-dorff, with another woman. What kind of a husband is that?

Accused : Not a very good one.

Public Prosecutor : Yet for his sake you were prepared to betray your solemn obligations as a citizen of the Republic?

Accused : The children were glad to see him.

In his summing-up the prosecutor spoke at length of the duty laid on every citizen, without exception, to obey the authorities at all times; and of the dangers to the state that would result if people were allowed to put their "private predilections" above the necessity to safeguard public order. He also urged the judge not to allow his natural concern for the wellbeing of the accused's children to dispose him towards leniency. The children in question would be taken into care and brought up to be loyal and dutiful citizens of the state. This was more than could be said of them if they were permitted to remain in the hands of "the criminal and irresponsible woman" before the court. The sentence: eighteen months, with hard labour, in a suitable penal institution. At that point, the report concluded, the prisoner broke down and was removed from the court.

Somebody dropped a book. The sound reverberated like a shot, under the great dome of the library.

I looked up vaguely. The noise of the explosion echoed in my ears. The light changed above the dome, and darkened again. What I had to do next had suddenly become quite clear to me. Of course! What else? The thought came like a reprieve. More: like an opportunity I had always unknowingly been waiting for.

At last I was going to take Josef Baisz by the throat. Yes! At last I could begin to feel for *him* that soft, loving tenderness which hitherto had been reserved only for his victims. I could even begin to pity him.

So I came here. I asked for ten days' leave before starting my new duties. Permission was readily granted to me. I did not return to the island. I spent one more night at home. Connie 'S Koudenhoof said he wanted to accompany me here; he too was entitled to a spot of leave, he'd enjoy the break, and so forth. I didn't mind. Why should I? What difference does it make?

It's all so obvious. All one's best ideas have that quality. Having struggled to arrive at them, the struggle one has gone through at once appears to have been quite unnecessary. *Well! How could I ever have imagined otherwise?* . . . Everyone knows those inner exclamations after the event, or after the moment of illumination.

I would never be discharged from the necessity of double-dealing and betrayal? I would always be serving the gods of falsehood and treachery? So be it. In that case the master who is within me has the vulnerability of all the others I have ever served.

I am going to prove it. I have the weapon. I have the will. But first I owe to all my masters a full, free confession of everything I have previously kept hidden, or have spoken of only in fragments to one person at a time. That too is inevitable, given the past. Nothing has been kept secret: not even the glee with which some of these memories have filled me.

Almost dawn. Tomorrow – today, that is – Connie and I are supposed to go down to the nearest railway station and make our way home. Who knows, he may be blamed for what I am going to do. That's his lookout. By the time he finds my body, however, in whatever nook or cranny of the mountainside I will have ensconced myself, my parcels of papers will be on the way to their recipients. I have been very methodical. I have the wrapping, the glue, the string. I know when the post is cleared from the local post-office and taken to the railhead – at which point it should be impossible to call it back. One has to think of everything. In any case, it is quite appropriate that I should be kept busy by such banalities to the very end.

The sky, I now see, has become quite distinct from the outlines of the mountains in the east. Not for the first time I try vainly, paradoxically, to imagine such a landscape vacated of my consciousness.

How carefully I have guarded this particular body! Guiding it across streets and down stairs, feeding and watering it, cutting its hair, trimming its nails, keeping it warm and dry, washing its hands after it has defecated, exercising it, putting it against other bodies for the satisfaction it could get from them, looking at it in mirrors . . . Poor thing, it has repaid my care in the only way it knows how: dumbly, obediently, performing its functions regularly, giving me pleasure in its simple pleasures. Now it becomes the last and most innocent of all my victims.

Many years ago, in the silence of my father's warehouse, I swore that I would make something of my life. Well, I have.

This.